HIS BIRTHDAY WISH

ELLE WATERS

ALSO BY ELLE WATERS

His Ever After Collection

His Christmas Love Song

His Coffee Shop Crush

His Fake Wedding Date

New Beginnings

Day Dreaming

For T.H.

ONE

JAKE HAD GONE to bed twenty-three years old and woken up a year older, but nothing had changed. Nothing ever changed.

He rolled out of the same bed he'd had since he'd outgrown his twin bed in tenth grade and his mother had sighed and bought a king to save them the trouble of having to haul yet another mattress up and down the stairs the next time he grew out of a bed. Jake had been six feet tall since eighth grade; he grew an inch a year after that until topping out at six-foot-five. The king was barely adequate, really.

He dressed in the same clothes he always wore, jeans, sneakers for his size fourteen feet that he had to special order. No stores in town carried his size. He pulled on a T-shirt which skimmed his navel and shrugged into an extra-tall flannel. He was glad his favorite one was clean, a soft blue-green pattern that forced his eyes to settle on looking green, rather than their usual odd mix of yellow, blue, and brown.

Jake swept his bangs over his too-high forehead and brushed his teeth. He gave himself a fake grin in the mirror he'd had to duck down to see his face in every day for the past decade.

Happy birthday to me. Before he descended the stairs, his neck craned to the side so he didn't bean himself on the way down, he made a wish. Everyone got a birthday wish, right? He made his wish half facetiously, half in hope. He wished for something to change.

"YOU HAVE ANY PLANS TONIGHT?" his mom asked. She'd made him carrot cake pancakes for breakfast. She made them every year.

"I have a shift that starts at seven." Jake sipped his coffee, took another bite of pancakes. They really were great, even if they were boring. His mom was a good cook. "And I have a few errands to run today."

"You getting together with any friends?" Liv asked lightly, sitting down at the small kitchen island next to him. He dwarfed the white wooden stool, while she perched on hers like a bird, the same dark brown hair and multicolored eyes that he saw every day, but on a slender five-foot-two body.

He avoided the inclination to roll his eyes at his mother. He might still live at home, but he didn't have to act like a teenager. "No." He didn't have any friends in Apple Vale. None his own age, anyway.

"You want me to cook something special for dinner?"

He felt bad that she was trying so hard to make today

nice. "No, thanks, Mom. I'm good. Maybe I'll bring home a pizza from Nero's or something."

"Okay, if you're sure."

"Sure. Thanks for breakfast."

"Happy birthday, Honey Cakes."

He gave in to the urge to eye roll at the endearment. "Mom."

"What? I gave birth to you twenty-four years ago; I'm allowed to call you Honey Cakes." She leaned over and kissed him on the cheek. "I have to stop by work for a while. See you."

"See you later. Love you."

"Love you, too."

He loaded the dishwasher, took out the garbage, and went back to his room. He'd avoided logging onto his socials and the forum where he was a moderator so far today, but he might as well check. There were probably a few birthday well-wishes he should respond to, and he wanted to make sure no one had bailed on their Grief Sucks shifts.

It took only a few seconds for his computer to boot up, lighting up with his desktop wallpaper—a picture of an Alex Ross Batman. His email and messages auto-loaded. He clicked on his message app, keeping his profile carefully invisible. He didn't want to have to respond to anyone right away.

He scanned the messages related to the online support group called Grief Sucks he'd joined as a member three years ago and was now a moderator for. That's where he'd met Chip, Raj, and Graham originally. They were all around the same age, and, like him, they were all unrepentant nerds who would rather interact with people safely from behind a computer screen than in the real world.

He'd gotten to know them individually, through the informal group therapy sessions that the forum hosted, then they'd started interacting in their own rooms, bonding over video games and anime. Chip was kind of a dick, but he had a good heart. Raj was the most well-adjusted of all of them. He had an actual girlfriend and a real job, so he was usually only around on the weekends.

Graham was...well, Graham was special. He was shy; he over thought everything. Sometimes Jake thought he spent his life waiting for the typing bubble to resolve into words when he was having a conversation with Graham. But it was always worth the wait. Graham was kind and funny. Jake looked forward to every time they hung out online.

It was Graham who suggested that Jake apply to be a moderator of the grief forum, and who'd gotten him thinking about getting certified as a grief counselor. Jake had taken his psych undergrad degree and started a master's program almost two years ago now. He was a few months away from graduating, and already had one part-time job, and another lined up. The first was at the Apple Vale retirement community slash nursing home, and the second was at the county hospital. Graham was his online confidant, the closest thing he had to a best friend, his favorite person to talk to when he woke up in the morning, and the last person he wanted to hear from before falling asleep at night.

Yes, okay, Jake was aware he had a crush on his

friend. He'd known it for about a year, since Graham started dating someone and Jake had confusingly moped over the news for days until he realized he was jealous.

When Graham and the guy broke up a few months later, Jake had planned to say something. He'd rehearsed it out loud, he'd even typed out a few versions in his notes app.

I know we've never met and we've never even spoken on the phone, but we've been hanging together online for three years and I think I might be a little bit in love with you well what do you think?

He'd stabbed the delete button until the words disappeared. What if Graham blocked him and Jake lost his best friend? He'd still have Raj and Chip, and the folks he'd met in his master's program, and his mom and Nana and the retirement home bunch.

But Graham wasn't replaceable.

Case in point—Chip was messaging him right now. The light next to his name was blinking with three unread messages. He could practically feel Chip's egregious use of exclamation marks through the screen.

Still, he ignored his friend in favor of clicking over to his chat with Graham, but nothing had changed. It was left to the last exchange they'd had—two days ago.

Graham: Your birthday is coming up, right?
Jake: Don't remind me.
Graham: You're only turning 24. Dude. You know I'm older than you so don't go complaining. :)
Jake: It's just that everything feels so...repetitive.

Nothing changes. I don't need another reminder that a year has gone by and I'm the same person I always was.
Graham: I like the person you are.
Jake: You do?
Graham: Yes.

Jake had held his breath until he felt lightheaded after reading that simple one-word response. Now was his chance. He should say something. He typed out the next two sentences before he could stop himself.

Jake: I like you, too. Maybe we should meet up sometime?

And that was it. He'd put it out there and Graham had immediately disappeared from the server, just as Jake had been afraid he would. It had been radio silence ever since.

Jake swallowed down the unwelcome sensation that he might cry. Graham must have had his reasons. Maybe he was just busy. It had happened before, when real life got hectic, and Graham dropped off the radar for a few days at a time. But he always came back.

For a distraction, if nothing else, he clicked on his conversation with Chip and was immediately assaulted by so very many exclamation points.

Chip: Happy b-day, J-man!!!!!!!
Chip: The big 24!!!! How does it feel to be almost able to rent a car??!!

Chip: I have the best birthday present for you. But you gotta be home to get it, so.
Chip: Jake!! Wake up!!
Chip: Seriously, you are going to want this present!!!!!

Jake rolled his eyes and figured he might as well get this over with.

Jake: Good morning, Chip. Thanks for the birthday wishes.
Chip: There you are! Okay, so I got you something for your birthday and I think you're really going to like it but you have to be home to get it!
Jake: What, like to sign for it?
Chip: Sort of. I think you're going to want to be there and not your mom, if you know what I mean.
Jake: I actually have no idea what you mean.
Chip: You know how you're 24 and still a virgin?
Jake: Jesus Christ, Chip. Fuck you.
Chip: No, no, it's good. I figured out what you need. I know there's no one for you in Hicksville, NY wherever it is that you live, but you're only like two hours from NYC, so I figured there'd be someone who would travel, and I found this guy, and he's super hot, like I think he's hot, so he must be hot, and he's going to be there soon, so just...you're welcome!!!!

Jake wished he had indulged in a second cup of coffee with his pancakes because he tried to make sense of Chip's message and just...couldn't.

Jake: Seriously, what the fuck are you talking about?
Chip: I got you a hooker!!!! His name is J.R.
Chip: Happy birthday!!

Jake had many regrets in life. He regretted the time he ate two funnel cakes, a corn dog, and a blue slushee, and then got on the Gravitron at the summer carnival. He regretted not spending more time fishing with his dad before he got sick. He regretted that he'd accidentally seen the second Matrix movie before the first. But at that moment, he had never regretted anything more than telling Chip that he was a virgin, blurted out one night when his mom had been out of town and Jake had lamented the fact he could go out and buy a six-pack to get mildly drunk on but had never had sex.

He'd had a Post-it taped to the wall behind his computer ever since—**No Drunk Messaging with Chip!** He now, belatedly, also regretted giving Chip his address so he could send him a vintage copy of *A Lonely Place of Dying* that he'd found at a flea market. It was Jake's favorite. Okay, maybe Chip wasn't the worst.

But a hooker?

He was about to launch into a rant telling Chip that he better fucking be kidding because there was no way that Jake was losing his virginity to a New York City hooker that Chip had picked out and—*ugh*—paid for, when the doorbell rang.

TWO

JAKE SERIOUSLY CONSIDERED pretending to not be home as the doorbell rang a second time. He could just not answer and whoever was on the other side of the door would go away and he would happily die a virgin. After killing Chip first, of course.

But he was too curious to let whoever was at the door simply disappear. He went downstairs as quietly as he could, which wasn't very. His mom had likened his gait around the house to that of a herd of mustangs on more than one occasion.

He bypassed the front door to sneak a glance out of a side window. A light-skinned man stood on the porch, one hand in his jeans pocket, the other hovering over the doorbell. He wore a broken-in jean jacket over a plain dark gray button down, and his face. Um. His face was sort of ridiculously good looking, to borrow a phrase.

Jake clocked the full, pretty lips, the prominent, straight nose. He couldn't tell what the guy's eye color was from this angle, but he had sandy brown hair with a bit of a fade going on with short sides and longer on top. Jake guessed he was probably in his late twenties. He could have been a model.

Or a hooker.

Whatever. Jake didn't judge. And this guy was basically exactly his type. Maybe Chip knew Jake better than he thought. Still, it took every ounce of Jake's courage to open the door.

The guy—Chip had said his name was J.R., like a cowboy or something—looked surprised at the door opening after such a long delay. "Jake?" His voice was low and a little scratchy. He cleared his throat immediately, as if he wasn't used to talking. "I'm —"

"I know who you are," Jake said. He wondered if he'd been able to keep the embarrassment out of his voice.

"Oh." J.R. licked his lips. His beautiful, pillowy, blush-pink lips. Jake dragged his gaze back to the guy's eyes. They were green. But not just any green, fresh-crayon-out-of-the-box-green. "I know you must be surprised. I didn't exactly know how to...and then Chip—"

"Please don't talk to me about Chip right now." Jake would have to devise some very specific way of getting back at Chip for this debacle.

J.R. smiled. "Fair enough." There was a pause. "Uh, can I come in?"

"Come in?" Jake hesitated. Come in, like, to deflower him? Was that how this worked?

"Or not, I guess." Half of J.R.'s mouth curved up ruefully. "To be honest, I kind of thought you'd be happier to meet me."

"Oh, sorry," Jake said, his innate politeness kicking in. Had he offended the hooker by not inviting him inside? "It's just that I wasn't expecting this—you."

"Look, you're right. I'm sorry. I get that this is weird. I just thought—why not? We're not getting any younger, are we?"

Jake let out a short laugh. He didn't know this guy from Adam, but he couldn't argue with that. It was his birthday, after all. "True. Yolo and all that."

J.R.'s laugh exposed sharp white teeth and made his eyes crinkle up a bit. It was really causing problems for Jake's moral compass that the guy Chip had hired to have sex with him was so damn gorgeous.

"Exactly, yolo." Then J.R. stepped right into Jake's space, wrapped his arms around Jake's shoulders, and hugged him.

Jake froze. When was the last time someone he wasn't related to had hugged him? He hadn't been hugged by someone who was almost as big as him since before his dad—well. J.R. was no gargantuan like himself, but he easily topped six feet. He smelled good, fresh and clean like soap, and he knew how to hug, firm and warm. Jake's heart stuttered a little at the unfamiliarity of being touched like this.

J.R. let go slowly. He rocked back, restoring a socially acceptable amount of personal space. He stood there, staring at Jake with an expectant look. Jake was at a loss. As much as part of him wanted to say fuck it and lose his virginity in broad daylight while his mom was at work to J.R. the Manhattan cowboy hooker, the rest of him proceeded with his usual defense mechanism

when faced with a situation out of his comfort zone—
he ran.

"You know what? I was just heading out to do some
errands, so unfortunately I can't ask you in," Jake said. He
grabbed his keys from the bowl on the table at the foot of
the stairs. With his long arms, he barely had to lean to
reach. In a second, he had the front door shut and locked
behind him. "I have a bunch of stuff to do today. Yeah, I
was actually on my way out and—"

"Can I come with you? Keep you company?" J.R.,
rather than taking the graceful exit Jake felt he was offering, seemed kind of excited at the prospect of errands.
Maybe it was a by-the-hour thing and he wouldn't get his
entire fee if he didn't spend at least some time with Jake?

The part of Jake that had been willing to consider
going through with using J.R.'s services also didn't want
to have to say goodbye to the beautiful man. Jake was a
virgin, not a masochist. It was something different,
anyway, and hadn't he just been lamenting the fact that
nothing ever changed?

"Um. Sure, you can come." Jake winced at his choice
of words. "I mean, my truck's in the garage. Let me get it
out." He hit the clicker on his key ring and the old metal
garage door slowly lifted to reveal a vintage Ford F-100.

J.R. whistled. "Nice ride. 1970?"

"'69," Jake said. Then he winced again. "She was my
dad's," he said quickly. "I'll be two seconds."

"Take your time."

He climbed into the driver's seat, started up the truck.
The engine whined a little as it warmed up. Jake spotted
J.R. in the side view mirror, watching the truck with his

head cocked to the side as if he was listening for something. He was really a handsome man. And instead of taking him to bed, Jake was taking him to run errands.

Jake clunked his forehead on the steering wheel. He couldn't deny that he was just the tiniest bit pathetic. No wonder he was still a virgin. A super-hot guy had literally been delivered to him on his doorstep, and he still couldn't seal the deal.

As he reversed the pickup down the short driveway, he had to admit to himself it wasn't just the fact that losing his virginity to a prostitute seemed kind of icky, and it wasn't the legality of the thing.

It was Graham.

Jake couldn't fathom being physically intimate with someone else when he felt the way he did about his friend.

His friend who had left him hanging for two days. Who hadn't even messaged him on his birthday. Before he could stop himself, Jake opened up his phone, willing there to be a new message from Graham. But there was nothing. He ignored the light next to Chip's name. Chip could fucking wait.

Jake cranked the window down, called out to J.R. "Hop in."

J.R. grinned, came around the passenger side and swung himself onto the bench seat, buckling in. "This is some ride. Pretend you don't see my Civic parked on the street there, okay?"

Jake laughed. "A Civic is better for the city, though, right? I'd probably be better off with something a little more economical, but I can't let go of this old thing."

"Old she might be, thing, she's not."

"My dad called her Beauty," Jake said, then he froze. It wasn't like him to talk about his dad with strangers. But there was something about J.R. Maybe it was because he wasn't someone from Apple Vale who'd known his dad, or maybe it was because after whatever weirdness that was today was over, Jake would never see him again.

"Beauty, huh? It fits. You might want to check the belts, though. I thought I heard a little squeak when you got her going."

"Oh, yeah?" Jake had done his best to take care of the truck these last few years, but he was no mechanic. "Thanks for the tip."

"'Course," J.R. said. "So, where to first?"

"Uh." Jake had planned to take care of a few things today. He hadn't planned on doing them with an audience, however. "The bank, I guess?"

"Sweet. Banking. Totally fun birthday activity. Happy birthday, by the way."

Jake slid his gaze over to J.R., who was looking at him with a strange, private smile. He was about to ask how J.R. knew it was his birthday when he realized Chip must have told him as part of the, er, hiring process?

"Thanks."

He drove on autopilot to the bank, while J.R. silently watched the town of Apple Vale, such as it was, pass by outside the window.

Jake tried to think of neutral conversation topics, but he wasn't used to making small talk with people in real life who were less than fifty years older than him. J.R. didn't seem to mind, or maybe he figured he wasn't getting paid to chat. Either way, they arrived at the bank a minute later in silence.

"You want to stay here? I just have to deposit a check."

"Yeah. I'll—sure. I'll stay here." J.R. looked sort of disappointed, but what was Jake supposed to do—bring him with him to the ATM?

Jake hopped out, jogged to the vestibule, and took care of depositing his paycheck from the retirement home —they weren't set up for direct deposit no matter how many hints he dropped that they were about two decades behind the times in their payroll processing. He took out some cash, too, which he rarely did. He did most of his shopping online, but maybe he was expected to tip? Not that he was going to take J.R. up on anything he might offer.

The urge to bang his forehead against something hard returned. This was a ridiculous situation, and J.R. was, perversely, not making it any easier by being so nice and chill. Not to mention hot like burning. If he'd been an asshole, it would have been a lot easier to send him away. Jake couldn't help thinking that his birthday wish for something to change was coming true. Which just went to show you had to be careful what you wished for.

His thoughts turned, as they had what felt like every ten minutes since he'd been left hanging in their chat, to Graham. What was he doing? Was he ever going to come back online? It wasn't like him to be deliberately cruel. Jake checked his phone again as he walked slowly back to the truck. Nothing.

J.R. watched him curiously as he got back behind the wheel. "You must be getting a ton of birthday spam."

"Uh. I guess." Jake had ignored all of that, but J.R. was right, he'd have to check in later. He could do it while he was on his Grief Sucks shift that night.

"So, I know you have stuff to do, but I got up super early this morning to drive here. Is there someplace I could grab a cup of coffee?"

"Oh, yeah, of course." Jake felt like a jerk. "How about some food, too?" he suggested.

"I could eat," J.R. said.

Suddenly, Jake was starving. "Yeah, me too." It was still a little early for lunch, but he was basically hungry 24/7.

"Let me buy you lunch," J.R. said. "Where do you like to go around here?"

"I can't let you buy me lunch," Jake said, instead of answering. He started up the truck, noticed that whine again. J.R. was right; he should take it to Terry to look at. He decided lunch at the Apple Pan was a safe bet, so he hooked a right and headed for his favorite diner.

"Sure, you can, it's your birthday. It's, like, against birthday rules to pay for yourself. Besides, I know you weren't expecting me, and I feel kind of like I messed up your whole day by just showing up here. I just—I—" J.R. ran a hand through his hair, disturbing the longer part on top. Didn't make him any less attractive, of course, unlike when Jake didn't brush his hair and it looked like he'd stuck his finger in an electric socket. "I—um. I guess I thought I'd show up, and we'd just—I don't know. I'm an idiot." He sighed and looked out the window instead of at Jake.

Jake's heart lurched at J.R.'s sigh. He sounded down.

Was he just starting out? Maybe he hadn't had that many clients and was as out of his element as Jake was. "Hey, no, you're not an idiot. I'm sorry. I'm just not used to spending time with people in real life." He cringed after he said it, but who was he trying to impress? He'd never see J.R. after today, anyway. "I might be a little rusty at the human interaction thing."

J.R. turned his head at that, and got that soft smile on his face again, the one that made Jake's stomach feel weird, as if he'd missed a step on the stairs and was about to fall. "Yeah. I get that. I guess that's why I'm here."

Jake let out a short laugh. Yeah. If Jake had real life friends or a real life boyfriend, J.R. would most definitely not be here. But the amazing thing was, J.R. seemed to want to be with Jake, as awkward as it all was. "Okay, you can buy me lunch, but only because it's my birthday."

J.R.'s small smile turned into a full-on grin. "Deal."

THREE

IT WAS STILL EARLY ENOUGH to grab a booth at the Apple Pan before the lunch rush. Jake slid into his side of the booth while peering down at his phone.

"Why do you keep looking at your phone?" J.R. asked.

"Sorry. Bad habit." Jake tucked the device into the pocket of his jeans, reached for the menu, even though he always ordered the same thing. It wasn't likely that Graham had messaged him in the ten minutes since he'd last checked, but he couldn't seem to help himself. Not for the first time, he considered if he'd be better off putting more effort into relationships with people in the real world and spending less time online.

He was tired of going through life hoping for something that was never going to happen. The fantasy that Graham was going to wake up one day and realize that his quirky online pal Jake was The One was just that—a fantasy that he needed to get over. Move on from. He frowned. He wasn't the greatest at moving on.

"So, what's good here?" A lock of hair fell into J.R.'s

eyes as he inspected the menu; he pushed it away with capable-looking hands.

"I always get the burger and fries," Jake said. He glanced at the options. Maybe he should try something different. "But today I'm thinking maybe a French dip?"

J.R. made a face at that. "The bread gets so soggy."

Jake couldn't remember if he'd ever actually had one. He considered tuna—but then he'd have tuna breath, which wasn't necessarily relevant, but— "The burger is fantastic. I could get a salad instead of fries."

"No, because I'm getting a burger with fries and if you get a salad, you'll end up eating half my fries and I don't share fries."

Jake laughed. "You don't share fries? What, is it against your religion?"

J.R. grinned, showing off those white teeth again. "Oh, most definitely."

Jake's gut felt warm whenever J.R. smiled. "What about dessert? Do you share dessert?"

J.R. narrowed his eyes. "What do you think?"

Jake wanted to snap back something witty and flirty and get J.R. to smile again, but he was out of his element. "No?"

"Only if properly motivated."

Jake didn't have a chance to figure out what J.R. meant by that because Liana came to take their order. J.R. indicated that Jake should go first, so he somewhat sheepishly ordered a burger. And fries.

"And coffee," he added. He didn't really need the caffeine, but he remembered J.R. requesting coffee.

"Same," J.R. said simply, handing the menu back to Liana with a polite smile.

"You two boys are easy. Not to mention easy on the eyes." Liana's gaze flicked over J.R. appreciatively. "Jake—who's your friend?"

Jake had known Liana for years. Her younger sister Rachel had been in his class at Apple Vale High. Since he only ever came in alone or with his mother, he supposed her curiosity was natural. Not to mention, J.R. was objectively more attractive than anyone in town. But how on earth was Jake supposed to introduce him?

"I'm—" J.R. started, but Jake cut in.

"A friend from out of town," he blurted. "It's my birthday." It wasn't as if he'd thought J.R. was going to come right out and say why he was there, but deflecting seemed like a good idea.

"Well, happy birthday! Good thing you told me—now I can give you ten percent off. You're the same age as Rachel, right? Twenty-four? Did you hear she just got engaged?"

Jake made polite noises while Liana launched into a description of Rachel's engagement ring and the fiancé and how they were looking at Atkins Farm for the reception. He threw an apologetic look at J.R., who smiled as if he thought the whole thing was charming.

"...they met online, which I know is pretty common, but still, when Rachel told me I was like 'how do you know he's not an axe murderer or like one of those weird conspiracy theory people' but apparently that's how it's done these days."

J.R. lifted his eyebrows and gave Jake another one of

those soft smiles that made it seem like they were sharing a joke. Only Jake hadn't been let in on it.

"I don't know, meeting online isn't that strange," J.R. said, still looking at Jake. "I've met some of my best friends that way."

Jake attempted a laugh, but it came out strangled and then he held his breath until Liana finally ran out of steam and left to put in their order.

"Sorry about that," Jake said.

"About what?"

"I don't know. In Apple Vale everyone's kind of up in everyone else's business."

J.R. shrugged. "It's nice. I miss small town life sometimes."

"You don't like living in the city?" Jake had been to Manhattan a few times over the years, and he always enjoyed it for about six hours until the noise and the crowds and the lack of sunlight started getting to him. He hadn't exactly planned on staying in Apple Vale his entire life, but Manhattan was a whole other extreme.

"Where I live is pretty okay. It's walkable, and the T's right there, so that makes it easier."

Jake felt his eyebrows come together in confusion. That was weird. Didn't they call it the subway in New York? The T was what they called the subway in Boston.

Thinking about Boston made him think of Graham. And that made him want to check his phone. Again. He drummed his fingers on the table instead of reaching for it.

"So, what else is on your to-do list?" J.R. asked. "Grocery shopping? Returning some overdue library books?"

It felt like the handsome man was teasing him, but not meanly. Jake shifted in his seat, embarrassed to tell him, even though he had no reason to think he would make fun.

"Well, I was going to stop by the animal rescue center. I volunteer there sometimes, but I'm going to be working more in a few weeks, so I need to tell them to take me off the schedule, at least until I get the hang of my new gig."

"The gig at the hospital?" J.R. asked.

"Yeah," Jake answered slowly. How much had Chip spilled to this guy about his life? He shook it off. "I start in about a month. Part-time, but between that and my other job at the retirement home, and other stuff, I'll have to be careful not to double book myself."

"Wow, I didn't realize how busy you're going to be," J.R. said, as if the news was making him think.

Again, Jake felt like he'd missed something, but then Liana arrived with steaming mugs of coffee, and he was distracted by the way J.R. pursed his lips to blow across the surface of his.

"What about you?" Jake said, when J.R. looked up and caught him staring.

"What about me?"

Jake felt his cheeks heat a little. He really hadn't thought the question through. "Are you busy...with work?" Since the likelihood of a sinkhole erupting in the middle of the Apple Pan was infinitesimal, he willed the blush on his cheeks to go away and accept whatever J.R.'s response was as if he had a shred of cool.

"Pretty busy, gearing up for the end of the year."

The end of what year? It was early May. Jake was going to ask for clarification, but then J.R. took a sip of his coffee. His upper lip came away pink and a little wet and his tongue peeked out of his mouth to lick it dry. Jake followed the motion, then hastily looked down at this own coffee as if that would make him forget that the man sitting across from him was basically sex on legs.

"Right." Between the coffee and J.R.'s tongue and the confusing mix of want and fear and frustration that was building in Jake's stomach, he was barely following the conversation at all.

"So, after we go to the animal shelter and break the bad news to them, is there anything else that you absolutely have to do today, or could I talk you into letting me come over for a while?"

Jake choked on his sip of coffee. He coughed, the acid and the heat burning his throat. J.R. looked concerned. "Hey, are you okay?"

Jake nodded, still coughing. He put up a hand. "I'm—" *Cough.* "—fine. Coffee down the wrong pipe."

"That sucks. Maybe switch to water," J.R. suggested sympathetically. He pushed Jake's water glass toward him.

Jake momentarily wished he could drown himself in the glass of water. But he hadn't resigned himself to dying a virgin just yet. He took a sip to steady himself.

"Come over?" he repeated, his throat scratchy.

"Yeah, you know, I feel like we need to talk." J.R. turned slightly pink after he said the words.

"We are talking," Jake said blankly.

J.R. shifted in his seat. "Well, I thought we could use more privacy."

Liana appeared at that moment to slide identical plates in front of each of them. "If you have any room for dessert, you say the word. We've got a wicked banana cream pie. I might even dig up a candle for the birthday boy."

"I hate bananas," Jake said at the same moment J.R. said, "Jake hates bananas."

Liana lifted her eyebrows and smirked. "Well, I'll have to see what else we got. Enjoy your lunch."

Jake was too stunned to be embarrassed by her knowing glance as she walked away. "How do you know I hate bananas?"

J.R. already had a mouthful of burger, so Jake had to wait while he chewed and swallowed to answer. "You told me."

Jake was starting to think he was being played. Was this some weird stalker he didn't know he had? "I don't think so."

"Yeah, remember when Raj was looking for pancake recipes so he could make his girlfriend breakfast for their anniversary, and I gave him one for banana pancakes and you spent like five minutes listing all the many ways you dislike bananas?" He took another bite of burger as if he hadn't just taken out a grenade in the middle of the diner and pulled the pin out with his teeth.

Jake looked at his plate, then back at J.R. He was beginning to suspect that this wasn't J.R. at all. He got out his phone. There were still no messages from Graham. He had four unread messages from Chip, however. He tapped on the screen, a sick feeling welling up in his chest.

Chip: You'll thank me for this one day, J-man!!!
Chip: Oh shit, he just messaged me that there's traffic or something and he's going to be late.
Chip: Like two hours late? Something about a logging truck on the interstate.
Chip: Whatever! It'll be worth the wait. Trust me. Have fun!! ;-)

Winky face. Fucking winky face.

Jake slowly looked up from his phone and stared at the man across from him. "Graham?"

FOUR

J.R.—GRAHAM?—THE person sitting across from him swallowed his bite and answered laconically. "Yes?"

Yes. As if he hadn't upended Jake's entire world with one syllable.

Jake dropped his eyes immediately, focusing somewhere in the vicinity of his fork. He couldn't—what was he supposed to—this was *Graham?* He forced himself to look back up again, but it was almost like trying to look directly at the sun.

It had been hard enough to interact with him when Jake thought he was just a good-looking stranger who was being paid to spend time with him. But it was *impossible* to look at him now that he knew the extraordinarily beautiful man also happened to be his best friend and the object of his secret desire.

He threw himself out of the booth, heart beating fast, mumbled something about the restroom, and fled. He banged through the swinging gray doors in the back of the diner and entered the single stall men's room, collapsing against the back of the door, trying to breathe.

All morning he'd been in the presence of his best friend, and he hadn't even known. How was that possible? He and Graham had spent countless hours talking online, chatting and joking, even sometimes watching so-bad-they're-good movies at the same time and trading snarky messages with each other.

Graham knew about his dad, about how losing him had been so hard Jake hadn't known what to do with himself until he'd stumbled onto the Grief Sucks group and found Graham in the process. Graham had been in the group for a reason, too. He'd lost someone close to him, and he'd told Jake that connecting with other people going through the same thing had helped him, which is why he'd stuck around Grief Sucks as a moderator. Graham had never told him who, exactly, he had lost, and Jake had never asked. They weren't supposed to if the group member didn't volunteer. But that didn't matter. The things that Jake didn't know about Graham didn't matter at all. He liked him because of what he did know.

And now he'd met him, in person, for the first time, and he'd messed it up. He'd screwed up the most important first impression of his life by assuming the beautiful man was a hooker. Jake spared a baleful thought for Chip over the entire debacle, but he knew it wasn't Chip's fault. He was the fuck up. He was the one who was so socially inept he didn't even recognize his best friend when he was right in front of his face.

No wonder Graham had been acting weird. He probably thought Jake was a head case. What was he going to do?

He leaned heavily against the bathroom door. The first thing he should do was apologize for the mix-up. But then he'd have to explain what he'd thought, and he'd have to explain Chip, which was doable, since Graham knew Chip, too. But how could he possibly ask Graham to give him another chance? He wouldn't be surprised if Graham just got back in his Civic and drove back to Boston and gave up on...whatever it was that brought him here in the first place.

Why *had* Graham come here? It was easily a four-hour drive from Boston, where Jake knew Graham was a teacher, to Apple Vale. Graham said he'd gotten up early to make the drive. Why?

He scrubbed a hand over his face and lurched over to the mirror above the sink. He looked peaked and feverish at once. He splashed some cold water on his face and tried to pull himself together. So that was Graham in that booth. So what? Graham was his friend. It didn't matter that he had apparently been cologne-ad gorgeous all this time. It was just Graham.

Jesus. It was *Graham*. Jake looked himself in the eye and said miserably, "I don't think I can do this."

Somehow, he made it back to the table, where Graham—god, he still stumbled over the name every time it came to him—was waiting. He'd eaten about half his burger and their coffees had recently been refilled.

"Everything okay?" his friend asked.

Jake shuffled back into his seat, keeping his gaze on the table. "Okay? Yeah. Of course. Why wouldn't it be?"

"I don't know, I just—look, maybe it wasn't such a great idea I had to show up out of the blue. I totally get if this is weird for you, and I can skedaddle."

Jake looked up at that. "Skedaddle?"

Graham blushed a little. "Sorry, a word left over from my childhood. I can scoot. You know, take off."

That was what he'd been afraid would happen, that Graham would leave because Jake was too pathetic to be around. "No, no. Please don't...skedaddle."

Graham smiled. "You sure?"

"I'm sure." Jake tried to sound firm. "Why did you decide to show up? I haven't heard from you in a couple of days." He decided not to mention he'd been obsessively checking his messages ever since Graham went silent.

"Well, that's kind of what I wanted to talk to you about." Graham glanced around the diner. It had filled up with the Saturday lunch crowd, and the noise level was increasing. Liana was running around, and Jake realized he hadn't eaten anything yet. As if reading his mind, Graham nodded at Jake's plate. "Why don't you finish up and we can talk later."

"Okay." Jake took a bite. Even lukewarm, the burger tasted good. Sometimes the reliable thing was still the best. Graham followed his lead, and they ate quietly for a minute. "So, are we not allowed to talk at all—or?"

Graham grimaced. "I guess maybe I'm not the best at this human interaction thing, either."

"That, I highly doubt," Jake said. "You're a teacher. You deal with people all day."

"Mostly twelve-year-olds. Twelve-year-olds I can

handle. It's grownups that are a pain in the ass to deal with."

Being around middle schoolers all day was something Jake was pretty sure he wasn't cut out for.

"I don't know if I could handle twelve-year-olds, but I have to agree, the older folks at the retirement home are much better company than most of the people I grew up with."

"So, between us we have the preteen set and the senior citizens covered. That's not so bad." Graham finished his burger and picked up his napkin.

Jake tried not to watch him wipe his mouth and failed. At least he wasn't having as much trouble looking at his friend now. Maybe he could do this after all. "But by this logic we shouldn't be able to talk to each other."

"You don't seem to have trouble talking to me online," Graham pointed out.

"You, either. Although sometimes it does take you a really long time to respond."

Graham cringed. "You noticed that?"

"Dude, sometimes I can make an entire sandwich in the time it takes for you to respond to 'what's your favorite M&M color?'" Jake put down his burger and switched to fries. They were a little cold, but still edible.

"That's because I have to check and make sure there's no secret code if I pick one color or another. I don't want to admit that brown is my favorite and then find out that means I'm admitting I'm secretly into tentacle porn or something."

Jake felt his face stretch into a grin. "You're googling

internet memes instead of answering the question? You are ridiculous."

"Hey, I've learned to be careful what I say online. The internet is forever." Graham seemed like he was kidding, but also not.

Jake wondered if he'd been burned in the past. Either way, there was something he had to know. "So, are you secretly into tentacle porn?"

"Wouldn't you like to know?" Graham waggled his eyebrows and waved to Liana, who appeared a moment later.

"Yeah, that's why I asked," Jake said under his breath. He wrenched his mind away from the direction it wanted to go in, which was wondering what exactly Graham's porn habits were. It was absolutely none of his business.

"What's up, boys? Need a box?"

"I think we're okay. You want dessert?" Graham asked him. It felt kind of strange that he'd taken over the interactions with the server, almost like they were on a date.

Jake shook his head.

"Just the check," Graham said, popping a smile at Liana, who fluttered and pulled the bill from her apron pocket. Graham had it back in her hand along with a credit card before Jake could even blink.

"Smooth," he said once Liana had left to ring them up.

Graham winked. Okay, well. *That* was the sexiest thing Jake had ever seen. Fuck. He'd thought he'd been into Graham before, but now it was all so, so much worse. Because Graham was just as nice as he was online, and just as funny, and just as weird. But he looked like *that*. And it was patently unfair, because Jake, with his oversized everything in his small- town, small-time life, could never be someone Graham would want to be more than a friend.

"So, animal shelter?" Graham asked once Liana had come back with the receipt. Jake noticed Graham left more than 20% for the tip. Dammit. Good tipping was such a turn-on, and Jake didn't need another reason to find his friend attractive.

"Animal shelter?" For a second, Jake had no idea what Graham was talking about. "Right, animal shelter. Yes. Let's go there. To the animal shelter."

Graham stood up, smiled easily. "Lead the way."

Jake tried to smile back, but he still had the feeling that it was only a matter of time before Graham realized that this was all a huge mistake.

FIVE

THE APPLE VALE ANIMAL SHELTER stood out by the highway, where it occupied a sprawling single-story building on a couple of fenced-in acres for the animals to play in. The outdoor space also gave them room to take in non-traditional animals like chickens and small domestic farm animals that, for one reason or another, needed to be placed in a new home. On this unseasonably warm May day, the scent of grass and manure from nearby farms mingled with the perpetual exhaust fumes from the highway.

Jake parked the truck in a visitor space, explaining what he typically did during his volunteer shifts as they got out of the vehicle. Graham had taken off his jacket on the ride and left it behind in the truck. He rolled up the sleeves of his gray button-down to his elbows, exposing golden forearms dotted with freckles. Jake tugged his own flannel down. He was always warm. On another day he might have taken his flannel off, tied it around his waist, but he felt shy around Graham's perfection. No one needed to see his too-long arms sticking out of his faded T-shirt.

"Hey, Sarah," he greeted the woman with short salt-and-pepper hair behind the desk. "Is Carrie around?"

"Jake! I didn't think you were on today," Sarah said, glancing between him and Graham. "You wrangle us another volunteer?"

"No, this is my friend Graham. Graham, this is Sarah." It was getting easier to cope with the reality that his internet friend had appeared in the flesh, but it was still a little surreal.

"Nice to meet you," Graham said politely.

Sarah beamed at him. "So nice to meet a *friend* of Jake's."

Jake willed his face not to heat at the emphasis she placed on the word friend. He avoided looking at Graham, in the hopes he hadn't picked up on the innu-endo. "I need to talk to Carrie, if she's free."

"I think so. You can go on back. We just got three kittens that someone dumped at the park. She should be processing them now. Good news, though. Rocky got adopted. He's getting picked up later today. You can go say goodbye if you want."

"Okay, thanks." Jake used his keycard to let himself and Graham through to the back, where immediately the sounds of animals took over the quiet of the reception area. There were aisles of crates, and a full veterinary clinic at the end of the hall.

"Who's Rocky?" Graham asked as they made their way past a row of cats.

"He's an older dog that came in a few months ago

when his family moved into a place that didn't allow pets. I worried they wouldn't find a home for him. Most people want a puppy or at least a young dog. But he's a sweetheart. Aren't you, Rocky?" Jake turned a corner and stopped in front of a large crate with a shaggy retriever-mix inside. The dog had been lying with his head resting on his front paws, but as soon as Jake approached, he perked up and started panting happily. Jake smiled even as his stomach tightened. He was going to miss visiting Rocky, but he was so happy he was getting a permanent home.

"You want to take him out?"

Jake turned when he heard the voice of Carrie, the head vet. She was looking at him as if she understood his mixed feelings.

"Sure, if that's okay?" he asked Graham, who just shrugged.

"I'm up for whatever you want to do," he said easily. "It's Jake's birthday," he clarified for Carrie.

"Happy birthday!" Carrie said. "I didn't know. Jake's really the best," she said to Graham, while Jake unfastened Rocky's crate and attached a walking leash to his collar. "He's amazing with the animals, even prickly ones who don't seem to take to anyone."

"I'm not surprised," Graham said. "Jake's pretty amazing at anything he does."

Jake cut his eyes to Graham, who seemed to be completely sincere. It was a strange feeling, having Graham here to support him in person, after years of only experiencing his kindness virtually.

"You aren't on the schedule today, are you?" Carrie

asked. "I could have rearranged things since it's your birthday. You probably want to go out and celebrate with your boyfriend."

It took Jake a second to realize she meant Graham. "Oh, no," he started, planning to correct her assumption, but Graham interrupted him.

"Jake's not on the schedule, don't worry about that. He just stopped by because he's about to start a new job and won't be as available."

Carrie's mouth turned down. "Oh, dear. I mean, I'm happy for you, Jake. I knew you were almost done with your degree, so of course you'd be moving on to new things. I hope you can still squeeze us in from time to time."

"I'll try," Jake promised. He really would miss the animals. "I can probably do a shift a week, at least."

"You let me know which slot you want and it's yours. Well, I have some kittens to check out. Nice to meet you," she said brightly to Graham, then slipped behind the door of her office.

Jake gave Graham a wobbly smile. "Let's take Rocky for a run outside."

"Lead the way."

They had the yard to themselves, and Jake ran Rocky around in circles for a while, then he took him off the leash and threw an old tennis ball for him to fetch. The dog pranced around Jake's knees, slobbering all over his shoes until Jake relented and dropped down, rubbing his soft fur vigorously until he could swear Rocky was grinning from ear to ear.

"If you're such a dog person, why don't you have one

of your own?" Graham asked, squatting down next to them and taking over for Jake. He pet Rocky with strong hands, while Jake leaned back and tilted his face toward the sun.

"I had a dog growing up," Jake said. "Cocoa. She came from the shelter with that name. My mom liked it, so we never changed it. She was the best. Great company for an only child like me." He swallowed hard, remembering how happy Cocoa was to see him when he got home from school, how cozy it was to curl up with her on winter mornings. "When my dad got sick, she never left his side. And then he died, and she—she was like fifteen by that point, but I could barely remember a time before she was in our family. And she just went, three weeks after he did. In her sleep."

He remembered how he hadn't known anything was wrong at first when his mom came to tell him, because she looked sad, and she'd always looked sad in those dark months after his dad's death.

"Anyway, it was hard. It was like losing him all over again." He looked up. Graham was staring at him, eyes grave, even while he kept stroking Rocky's fur. "And I just —I don't know if I could go through that again."

They sat in silence for a minute. Even Rocky seemed to be extra quiet. When it came, Graham's voice was gentle, but his words pierced through Jake's defenses. "Not loving isn't going to stop you from hurting, Jake. I know that."

His chest ached with the sad certainty in Graham's voice, and he wanted to ask him what caused him to hurt, but he felt like the person next to him was almost a stranger, no matter how well they thought they knew each other before today.

"Well. Anyway. Maybe someday I'll be ready. In the meantime, it's a big responsibility to have a dog and I have enough on my plate with school and work and my mom and—whatever." He attempted a laugh. "You get the idea."

"Yeah." Graham looked a little sad for a second, but then Rocky licked his hand and he smiled. "I think he likes me better than he likes you."

"Like everyone else we've met today?" Jake said without thinking.

Graham's smile disappeared. "No. What?"

"Never mind. It's fine. I'm used to being kind of invisible around here."

"What are you talking about? Carrie thinks you're the best thing since sliced bread. Sarah, too."

"I guess." It was hard for Jake to see that when he felt so alone most of the time.

"Anyway, Rocky is clearly all about the belly rubs," Graham added, lightening the mood. "Aren't you?" He started talking to Rocky and scratching his belly. The dog wriggled happily, then launched himself at Graham's chest to lick wet stripes all over his face. Graham was laughing and trying to push him off, and Jake giggled at the sight of Graham with an armful of dog. He looked good, too, unsurprisingly. Jake never realized how sexy a good-looking man being inundated with dog kisses could be.

Finally, he took pity on Graham and grabbed Rocky's

collar. "Come on, let's give Graham some breathing room."

Graham sat up, still laughing, his cheeks flushed. "I'm covered in dog spit," he groaned.

"Poor baby," Jake teased. "You can clean up inside."

"Yeah, I'll do that while you take a minute with Rocky."

"Okay. Thanks." It was thoughtful of Graham to realize that saying goodbye to Rocky wasn't going to be easy. He'd gotten attached in the last few months, something he tried not to do, but it was hard not to sometimes. He watched Graham retreat inside, then knelt and gave Rocky a kiss on the top of his nose. He brushed his cheek along the soft fur on the crown of the dog's head. "Be good, okay? I'll miss you."

Jake blinked to keep himself from letting any tears fall. Graham was right. You could try not to love something, or someone, and you still ended up hurting.

After he got Rocky back in his crate and washed his hands, he found Graham talking to Sarah in the front. His face looked pink, as if he'd scrubbed it clean, and his shirt was a little wrinkled and there was a grass stain on one of Graham's knees. He looked more handsome than ever.

When Graham caught sight of him, the polite smile he'd had on his face transformed into something brighter. Jake felt the warmth in his chest slowly expand outward as he got closer to Graham. There was something about him that made him feel...different. Good.

He was in trouble. They said goodbye to Sarah, headed back to the truck. Before they got in, Jake asked the question that had been on his mind since Rocky's kiss attack. "You seem like a dog person, too. Do you have any?"

"I'd like to have one, but like you said, it's a big responsibility. Especially where I live, there's not much yard to speak of. It would mean a lot of walks." He looked at his shoes. "I always figured it would be easier if I had someone to share the work with."

Jake thought of the guy Graham had been dating last year. Had he not been a dog person? He wondered if Graham was seeing anyone now. He hadn't mentioned anything like that for a while, but they didn't tell each other everything. Clearly. The warm feeling he'd had a few minutes ago evaporated at the thought of Graham dating someone. Someone who he might want to get a dog with. The urge to object was so strong he had to stifle the words, even though he realized getting upset over a hypothetical dog-adoption situation was ridiculous.

He shook his head to clear it of nonsense. As if that would help. He dug out his phone to check the time, noticed he had a text from his favorite aunt wishing him a happy birthday. He smiled, glanced up, and Graham was looking at him with a funny look on his face.

"What?"

"It's just. When you smile. You have dimples. I didn't know. About them," Graham said, words oddly stilted.

Jake could practically feel the aforementioned dimples disappear as his smile slid into a frown. Were they a turn off? Was Graham repulsed by the way his cheeks carved into lines when he smiled? "I'm sorry?" he said uncertainly.

Graham laughed. "Man, don't apologize. They're—you're—" he broke off, and looked like he wanted to say more, but nothing came out. Jake had the sense he was seeing in real time what it looked like when Graham poised over his keyboard trying to resolve his response into words while those typing dots bounced on an endless loop.

Jake could wait.

And then his phone rang. Actually, legitimately rang, which meant it was either an emergency or— "Hi, Nana."

Graham's eyebrows lifted and his mouth closed. Jake turned away. He needed to be able to focus on his grandmother's words and not Graham's face.

"Thanks, Nana. No, I didn't forget...but now's not...um. Okay. Be there soon."

He shoved his phone back in his pocket and turned to Graham.

"Nana?"

"My grandma. She lives at the retirement home I work at. And she's insisting I come over so she can wish me happy birthday in person." They were only a few minutes away from The Vale; it would take more than half an hour to drive all the way to Graham's car to drop him off and then back again. Jake was about to offer anyway, but Graham spoke first.

"Well then, let's go see your nana."

SIX

THEY ARRIVED at The Vale a few minutes later. The generic name matched the rather nondescript building, a three-story white stucco rectangle lined all around by trees.

"You really don't have to come with me to visit my grandma," Jake tried, but Graham wasn't having it.

"No, no, I'm your shadow today. Where you go, I go." Graham's enthusiasm faltered. "Unless there's a reason you don't want your grandma to meet me."

"No, it's not that. I can't imagine this is what you had in mind when you came to visit me." Jake was still a little unclear on the exact reasons for Graham's visit in the first place, but he was trying to go with it. Ugh, being spontaneous was stressful.

He relaxed a little once they got through the doors and signed in at the front desk. He was here twice a week to run the community grief support meeting, and he usually spent a chunk of time before and after visiting with Nana and whoever else was in the common room, so he knew most of the residents by name.

"I think Elizabeth is in the atrium," Sid, the man at the desk, told him.

"I'll find her," Jake said. "Come on, Graham." They walked down the hallway and through French doors into the "atrium." It was more like a glorified enclosed patio with a few potted plants to give it the air of a greenhouse.

Jake's Nana was spraying water on a dilapidated orchid, headphones over her ears. He waved to her until she saw them and pulled the headphones down. She held up a finger. "Hold on, I have to turn off my podcast. I don't want to miss anything."

She got her phone out of the pocket of her jeans and pressed the screen. "There. Now, where's my hug?"

Jake leaned down to wrap his 5-foot-nothing grand-mother in a hug. She felt frail in his arms, but her build belied her inner strength. Nana was only in her late 70s, but she'd lived at The Vale for three years already. She had been happy enough to give up the headache of taking care of her own home once her husband had passed away, and she loved the community aspect of living with other people her age. Jake was glad she had access to good company, three nutritious meals, and health care on call twenty-four-seven. He'd worry about her rattling around alone in the old farmhouse she'd raised four children in.

"And you brought me a present!" she exclaimed once he let her go. "How did you know a handsome young man was just what I wanted? Jake, you shouldn't have. It's your birthday, not mine." She winked at Graham, who honest-to-goodness flushed red and stuck his hands in his pockets awkwardly.

"Nana, jeez," Jake said. "This is Graham. My friend from the grief forum."

"Of course, Graham, I've heard so much about you. I'm Elizabeth Crane; please call me Elizabeth. Let's sit." She indicated an ornate metal bench while she took a more comfortable looking chair across from it. "What have you boys been up to today? I didn't know you were expecting an out-of-town guest."

"I wasn't—" Jake started just as Graham said, "He didn't know I was coming—" and then they both fell silent when they realized they were talking over each other.

"It was kind of a surprise," Graham said finally, sitting down on one side of the bench. Jake took the other, being careful to leave as much room as possible between the two of them.

"I'll say," Jake muttered. Louder, he said, "I've been showing Graham around. We went to the Apple Pan for lunch and out to the animal shelter."

"And what do you think of our little town?" Nana asked.

"It's real homey," Graham said. "Kind of like the town where I grew up in Texas."

"A Texas boy? You came all the way here from the Lone Star State?"

"No, ma'am, I went to Boston for college a decade ago and never left. I live in Cambridge now."

"My late husband, Jonathan, Jake's grandfather, went to MIT on the GI Bill. I loved going to visit over the years. So pretty."

"I like it, especially when I can avoid the traffic."

"You know, it's wonderful of you to come visit Jake on his birthday. He spends so much time on that computer of his for school and his volunteer work, I worry about him getting out into the world and meeting people."

"Nana, I'm right here." Jake tried not to feel twelve years old.

"I just wish you'd take some time for yourself and go see something of the world. You've been living with your mother for twenty-four years. Don't you think she'd like a break from you?"

Jake knew his grandmother wasn't trying to be mean, but her words probed a part of himself that he'd struggled with for a long time. He'd planned to go to college out of state when his dad fell ill, and he couldn't leave because he didn't want to miss any time he had left with his dad. Then, afterward, it was too hard to think about moving some place new, especially when his mom seemed so drained, so sad. He started taking classes at the community college, and before he knew it, a few years had gone by. By the time he had his undergraduate degree, his mom no longer seemed as needy. He, on the other hand, felt woefully under-prepared to strike out in the world alone. Hence, his online life and his remote master's program. But he knew there was truth to what Nana was saying. He'd had the sense it was time he leave the nest. But taking that first step seemed nearly impossible.

"I suppose she would," is all he could say in response. He didn't look at Graham.

"You could start by visiting Graham in Cambridge. Couldn't he?" she asked his friend.

"I'd love nothing more," Graham said. His voice was low and serious, and Jake couldn't help peeking over at him. Graham's eyes were trained on Nana, however, and Jake couldn't pick up anything but sincerity from his face. If Graham was so enthused about Jake coming to visit, why had it never come up before?

"Anyway. It's none of my business," she said, as if she wasn't the nosiest grandma in New York state. "Graham, tell me a little more about yourself before I let you young-sters free to do whatever young people do these days."

Jake did roll his eyes at that. Nana was far from out of touch. He knew for a fact she was probably listening to a true crime podcast and would binge whatever was trending on Netflix later today. But Graham took the bait and started giving her a rundown of his life.

"I'm a middle school teacher, computers and year-book, and I coach track, too."

"And you're who we have to thank for getting Jake into this counseling business. He was at loose ends until he went back to school."

"Uh, I guess so?" Graham looked at Jake ques-tioningly.

Jake had never exactly told Graham how pivotal his help had been. "Well, you were the one who told me to get more involved with Grief Sucks, and it was really rewarding, so yeah, until then it never occurred to me it was something you could do as a career. I like helping people who are going through what might be the hardest thing they'll ever have to deal with."

He felt like a fraud, sometimes, because he still felt so much over the loss of his dad. But then he remembered that his experience and how he'd dealt with it helped him help others, and that made him feel like it was all worth it.

"I didn't realize," Graham said. "But that's really cool. I mean, it obvious you have a talent for it. Not everyone has the capacity to help people with heavy stuff like that."

"You've always been a sweet soul, Jake," Nana said. "Like my Jonathan. He was the most gentle man. Not like me, ornery bitch that I am." She laughed as Jake's jaw dropped.

"Nana!"

"Oh, don't look so shocked. You know you didn't get your sensitive genes from me. I think that's what made Jonathan and me a good fit—he saw past my crusty exterior and saw that I needed to be loved. And I stood up for him when he needed someone at his back. We were a good team." She looked past Jake as if she could see into the distance—into the past she shared with her husband, perhaps, or maybe toward a future where they'd be together again.

Jake had admired his grandmother for being proactive, moving on after becoming a widow, making a new life for herself at The Vale, but he wondered if what she wasn't doing was marking time. He thought about his mom, still young enough to fill her life up with more than just work and her adult son-slash-roommate. Had he been cramping her style these last few years? She'd never said anything, but suddenly he felt foolish. All her hints about trying to date or meet people his own age. He sighed. He didn't always feel like it but had to face the fact that he was an adult now. It was time for him to go.

"You okay?" Graham asked, when Jake sighed again.

"I'm fine. Just having some life-changing realizations."

Graham's eyebrows went up. "Really?"

Nana cackled. "Excellent. Birthdays are a good time to take stock."

"Yes, thank you, Nana. I'm so glad I came by so you could turn my life upside down and embarrass me in front of my friend."

"Anytime," she returned. "Now, I have your present here someplace." She looked around and then grabbed a small package wrapped in silver paper from behind a potted geranium. "Here it is."

"You didn't have to get me anything," Jake said, even as he was tearing into the paper like a kid on Christmas morning. A plastic card fell into his palm. "A gift card to Singer's Steakhouse. Thanks, Nana." The restaurant in the next town over was his favorite. "I'll use this to take you for lunch one day soon, okay?"

"I confess when I bought it that's exactly what I had in mind," she said, leaning over to kiss his cheek. "However, now I want you to use it to take Graham out for a nice dinner tonight."

"Oh." Jake looked at Graham. Was he even going to be around tonight?

"I never say no to steak," Graham said. "That's really thoughtful of you, Elizabeth. Thank you."

"Thank you for being a good friend to my favorite grandson."

"I'm your only grandson," Jake reminded her with a smile.

"Six granddaughters and one grandson. Maybe I'll

live long enough to see some great- grandchildren, too. Do you want kids of your own, Graham?"

"Uh—"

"We need to leave now," Jake said, standing up and giving Nana a quick hug goodbye. "Graham has endured enough for one day."

"Fine, ruin all my fun," Nana said, pouting melodramatically. "Don't be a stranger, Graham. You come visit next time you're in town."

"Yes, ma'am," he said dutifully, but he seemed slightly relieved to let Jake usher them back through the building and outside to the parking lot.

"Sorry—that went in a strange direction, but that's Nana for you."

Graham knocked his shoulder into Jake's. The split-second touch had Jake instinctively leaning in for more before he remembered they were just friends. Not to mention Jake had never had a boyfriend and didn't really know what the rules for casual touching were, anyway.

"I liked her. Thanks for letting me meet her," Graham said. "I'm learning a lot today, Jake."

"About my weird family?" he joked.

"Your family isn't weird. They love you."

"Yeah. I know. I'm pretty lucky, I guess."

"And besides, we're eating steak tonight." Graham checked his phone. "It's a little early yet, so we probably have time to run to the post office or pick up your dry cleaning first," he said dryly.

Jake laughed. It felt good that Graham could make jokes at his expense. They were getting along just as well in person as they did online. He hoped he didn't do something to screw it up, though if Graham could survive Nana's inquisition, he could probably survive most anything.

"I've never owned something that needed dry cleaning," he said.

"In that case, maybe we could go back to your house?" Graham suggested.

His house. Right. So they could talk. Jake suddenly remembered who else was supposed to be coming to his house. Maybe it was rude to leave J.R. hanging, but when no one answered the door, he'd get the picture and leave. No harm, no foul. Jake could just pay Chip back whatever he'd spent. On the other hand, if he hadn't shown up yet, Graham was the last person he wanted to explain J.R. to.

"I don't think—um." He wracked his brain for a non-dorky activity they could do to stay out of the house until he could be certain that J.R. had come and gone. In a flash of inspiration, he remembered something that might be up Graham's alley. "I want to show you something first, okay?"

Graham looked a little frustrated, but in the end he smiled. "I'm all yours," he said, and climbed into the passenger side of the truck.

Jake wished with whatever birthday magic he had left that that could be true.

SEVEN

"NO WAY."

Jake watched as Graham's expression morphed from confused to excited as they pulled into the train station parking lot to join the three dozen or so classic cars that were on display on one side of the lot.

Graham twisted excitedly in his seat to face Jake. "A car show?"

"They have it every other Saturday in the summer. It's not super formal—just a bunch of car geeks who want to show off. Figured you'd get a kick out of it." He'd forgotten that Graham was into cars, but his admiration of Beauty had reminded him—at least it had once he'd belatedly realized it was Graham doing the admiring and not a random guy.

Graham was grinning like a little kid. "Awesome."

They parked next to a shiny red Corvette Stingray and climbed out. Jake wasn't an expert, but at least he knew a Chevy from a Ford, thanks to his dad being a die-hard Ford man.

Graham led him down the first aisle of cars, smiling and nodding at the owners, some of whom were set up in camp chairs next to their babies. He stopped in front of a sky blue '60s Mustang to take a closer look, and Jake took the opportunity to look at Graham. He was less put together than when he'd first shown up on Jake's doorstep that morning. They'd had their share of adventures today, and it was a warm day. His hair had wilted and his shirt was wrinkled. He looked relaxed as he smiled and pointed out little details of the car and Jake was honestly not listening to anything he was saying. Instead, he marveled at the fact that Graham was here. With him. And he seemed *happy*.

"Oh cool, a Galaxy. Man, this thing is a boat," Graham exclaimed, as they walked by a giant black car.

"How did you get so into cars, anyway?" Jake asked.

"My dad, mostly. He traveled a lot for work, and he always brought me and my brother back a Matchbox or Hot Wheels. Sometimes he'd get me a nicer model. I still have a bunch of them lined up on a shelf in my bedroom like a five-year-old."

Jake could only imagine that Graham had been a cute little kid. "And you're something of a mechanic, right? Do you work on your car?"

Graham's excitement dimmed slightly. "Um. Yeah, some. I can change my own oil, simple things."

"Your dad teach you that stuff, too?" Jake's dad had tried to get him into cars, had even wanted him to take auto shop in high school, but he'd avoided it. Some of the kids who took shop were the same ones who bullied him for being gay. Once he died though, Jake regretted not paying more attention, lest he damage his dad's precious truck through negligence. Luckily, Terry at the shop in town took good care of Beauty when she needed something.

"No, actually. My. Uh. Mitch."

"Your Mitch?" Jake had never heard Graham mention a Mitch.

Graham cleared his throat. "Mitch. He was, uh. My college boyfriend. First boyfriend. First everything."

"Oh." There was something—or maybe several things —that Graham wasn't saying. Jake looked around. A few people were milling around looking at the cars, but no one within earshot. Still, he felt protective of Graham's privacy. "Should we go?"

"No, it's okay. I'm okay. I just—don't talk about him that much anymore."

Jake wasn't exactly sure why they were talking about one of Graham's exes now, but he could tell there was something else Graham wanted to say. He waited with patience he had cultivated over years of being Graham's online friend.

"He could take anything mechanical apart and put it back together better than new. He drove a motorcycle that he built himself."

Jake ignored the part of him that was jealous of Mitch, who seemed way more competent and cooler than Jake could ever hope to be. "And he taught you?"

"He showed me around an engine, yeah. Made fun of the tin can I was driving at the time, but it was all I could afford. He was a little older than me, and he taught me about a lot of things, including...yeah, including never get on a bike without a helmet." He ran a hand through his hair, mussing it further, and let out a heavy breath.

"Which is why it was such a shock when he died. He'd been drinking, and he got on his bike without his helmet, and he crashed." Graham swallowed and Jake could see his jaw tighten before he gritted out the rest. "We'd been fighting. A stupid fight about me going to grad school. We'd been together for four years and I thought he'd want to come with me to New York, but he wanted to stay in Boston." Graham fell silent and shuffled along to the next car unseeingly.

"Jesus, Graham. I'm so sorry." This was a side of his friend he'd never been allowed to witness before. "That's why you were in Grief Sucks. You lost Mitch."

"It was really hard for a while. I had a lot of guilt. I missed him. I stayed in Boston and did a different grad program just so I could feel like I was closer to him. It was dumb, in retrospect. Maybe it kept me from moving on." Graham looked up, met Jake's gaze with his clear green eyes. "But then I met you and I wanted to try. Moving on."

Jake was astonished. "I helped you with that?"

"You were just so honest and real and not afraid to be yourself, even when that person was a mess."

Jake quirked his mouth up. "Gee, thanks."

"I mean, at first, when you were really raw over your dad. But you got better. And it inspired me to get out there. Date again."

Jake's heart sank. So, he'd helped Graham and Graham had moved on by dating. That made sense. But it still made him sad that his hopeless feelings were destined to be crushed under Graham's boot when he finally met someone who made him happy. Someone cool enough to drive a motorcycle and clever enough to reassemble an engine, things Jake would never be.

"But then I realized—and I can't believe it took me this long—but I realized—"

"Watch out!" They'd been walking along the second aisle of cars. Jake hadn't been paying attention to any of them while he listened to Graham, but he noticed when a metallic pink hot rod started up and started backing out of its spot without looking where it was going. He put his arm in front of Graham, stopping him from walking into the car's path. Graham startled and stopped, looking from the car to Jake.

"Thanks. I didn't see it."

"I know." Only then did Jake realize his arm was touching Graham's chest. He dropped it quickly. He started talking again to cover up his embarrassment at being overprotective. "Thanks for sharing that with me, Graham. I'm sorry about Mitch. I'm glad I could help, even if I didn't know I was helping."

"Yeah. You know, that's what friends do. They help just by being there."

"Friends," Jake repeated. He had the rest of his life to wish Graham could think of him as more than a friend. For right now, he could be grateful he had his friendship. He smiled. "I'm really glad you came to Apple Vale, Graham."

"Really?" Graham looked pleased. "That's...that's good to hear."

They spent a few more minutes looking at the cars.

Jake declared his favorite to be a jade green BMW 2002. When Graham asked him why, he told him because it was stylish, but left out the fact that it was the same color as Graham's eyes.

When asked for his favorite, Graham pointed across the lot. "Beauty."

Jake laughed. "She's not in the show."

"But she's been cared for with love. And she's big enough for guys like you and me. That tiny BMW might be a tight fit for you, Stretch."

There was nothing but gentle teasing in Graham's voice, but Jake's shoulders hunched over anyway at the reminder that he was too tall. Graham was at least six feet, but Jake had a few inches on him.

"We need leg room," Graham went on. "Your truck is the perfect fit."

You're a perfect fit. Jake blinked away the thought. "I'm glad you like it."

"This was a lot of fun. And thanks for listening to me about Mitch. I had sort of been meaning to tell you about him for a while but...I don't know. The timing never seemed right."

"It's okay," Jake said neutrally. His heart hurt for Graham's loss, but he was glad to know about that part of his life. "So, you ready for steak yet? I don't think we'd need a reservation, but I could call ahead." They walked to the truck and got in.

"You know what, I'd really like to freshen up before dinner. I hope this doesn't sound strange, but I reserved a room at a motel for the night. Do we have time for me to go check in and take a shower?"

Jake was full of questions, but all he said as he pulled out of the parking lot was, "Sure. Sounds good. Let's go back to your car."

Graham seemed to sense Jake's confusion because he started to explain without Jake having to ask. "I just didn't think I'd want to turn around and drive all the way back to Boston in one day, so I figured I'd stay over, but since I didn't exactly tell you I was coming, I didn't want to impose on you. Is that okay?"

"Of course. It's too far to drive here and back to Boston in one day. I wouldn't want you out on the road late at night. Which motel?"

"Uh, Shady View Motel, something like that?"

Jake laughed. "I think you mean Shadow Brook Motel. Shady View sounds like a den of iniquity."

Graham joined in the laughter. "I hope I didn't accidentally reserve a by-the-hour room."

The reminder of what a person might want a by-the-hour place for sobered Jake up. He hoped by now that the mysterious J.R. had long since gone back to where he came from.

When he turned the corner onto the street he'd lived on his entire life, he scanned for anything out of place, but the only car that didn't belong there was Graham's dark blue Honda. He pulled into his driveway and left the truck there instead of pulling all the way into the garage.

"So, you want to meet me there, or—" Suddenly it seemed like a terrible idea to go through with eating a meal out with Graham. Lunch at the diner was one thing. Dinner at a steakhouse just had too much of a pre-prom date vibe. Not that Jake had gone to prom, but still.

"I could pick you up? Give me an hour?" Graham suggested brightly.

Jake looked at him for a long moment. How was this beautiful person who he cared about so much actually looking forward to having dinner with him? It didn't matter that it wasn't a date. It was still out of the ordinary for Jake. He refrained from pinching himself to prove it was really happening.

"I'll be here."

EIGHT

JAKE TORE upstairs and threw on the hot water in the shower. It always took a minute to heat up, so he checked his messages while he stripped out of his clothes. That was when he remembered he was supposed to have a two-hour shift moderating the Grief Sucks server starting at seven. They usually didn't have to do much, but there were occasional bad actors who had to be removed, or someone needed a referral for professional help, which the moderators always took seriously. He enjoyed being there, welcoming newbies and visiting with regulars, and in general giving people a place to vent or reminisce or retreat or laugh for a second of relief from whatever stage of grief they were going through.

But he couldn't make his shift and have dinner with Graham at the same time. He sat down at his desk and clicked on his messages. There was a new one from Chip.

Chip: How's it going? I want details!! Sort of. Wait, no details! Maybe keep it vague.

His icon had a green dot showing he was online. Good. Chip owed him.

Jake: I need you to take my 7-9 shift tonight

Chip answered within thirty seconds.

Chip: It's going that well! Am I a good friend or what??
Jake: No comment. Just, can you take the shift?
Chip: Because it's your birthday, I will cancel my plans to hate-watch Batman Begins and help you out!
Jake: Thank you
Chip: And then tomorrow you can give me the deets
Jake: That's not happening.
Chip: What? Come on!!

Jake took a deep breath and counted to twenty before answering.

Jake: We are going to have words. Tomorrow. Right now, I have to get ready for dinner.
Chip: That's my boy. Dinner!
Chip: Wait, dinner is a euphemism for sex, right?
Chip: Jake?
Chip: Bueller?
Chip: Fine, be that way.

Jake took the world's fastest shower, bent down to peer in the mirror to see if he needed to shave, decided it wouldn't make a difference one way or the other, and stopped in front of his closet. Shit. What was he going to wear? He'd been wearing his favorite shirt all day, and now it was dirty. The steakhouse wasn't fancy, but he wanted to look nice. Not *for* Graham, exactly. But it was his birthday, and it made sense he'd want to look nice on his birthday.

Okay, yes for Graham.

He found a pair of dark wash jeans that he rarely wore because they were a little tight, but maybe that wasn't a bad thing. He slipped those on over a fresh pair of boxer briefs, then agonized over his shirt choice for a while until he finally pulled on a plain white V-neck T-shirt. Then from the very back of his closet he grabbed one of his dad's jackets, an old dark blue blazer. James Crane had been Jake's height but fifty pounds heavier, so the jacket was a little big, but when Jake peered down into the bathroom mirror again and smoothed his hair, he thought he looked okay.

He grabbed his wallet and his phone and started downstairs before he did an about face and marched back to the bathroom. He'd forgotten deodorant. What a disaster that would have been; he was nervous enough as it was. Quickly, he took care of that detail and bounded noisily down the stairs.

The rest of the house was dark—it didn't seem like his mom had been there since she left that morning, which was fine, but a little strange. Maybe she'd stopped to do some errands after work. He texted her to let her know he was going out.

Long story but I won't be home for dinner. Don't wait up.

Don't wait up? What was that? He and Graham would probably have some food, maybe a beer, and then Graham would go back to the Shadow Brook Motel and Jake would come home and go to sleep in the same bed he'd woken up in. Nothing else was on the agenda.

Before he could decide if he should message her again to somehow play his text off as a joke, his mom replied.

Sounds good Honey Cakes. I'm out, too. See you tomorrow, ok?

Tomorrow? That was kind of weirdly specific, but he didn't have time to dwell because there went the doorbell again for the second time that day.

The first thing Jake noticed when he opened the door was that Graham looked like a million dollars after taxes. He'd fixed his hair and traded his gray shirt for a soft blue one and black jeans. The second thing he noticed was that he'd shaved, which immediately made Jake feel like a rube for skipping it. Not that it mattered. It wasn't like they were going to be kissing or anything.

Jake realized he'd been standing at the open door for kind of a long time without saying anything, but then again, Graham hadn't said anything either and was just standing there, looking right back at Jake.

"Can we have a do-over?" Jake said, breaking the silence.

"What do you mean?"

"This morning, when you showed up. I kind of want another chance to meet you for the first time." It had been nagging at him all day, the fact that the first time he'd seen Graham, the first time he'd touched Graham, he hadn't known that it was him. "Could we do it again?"

Graham didn't laugh at him or tell him he was being ridiculous. He smiled, and said, "Hi Jake."

God, he loved the way Graham said his name, kind of gruff but soft at the same time. "Hi Graham."

And then Graham stepped into Jake's space and hugged him, just like that morning, only this time Jake hugged back. Graham still smelled like soap and still felt firm and warm, but it was all so much more intense knowing it was Graham in his arms. He held on for a few seconds until he felt Graham shift and then they stepped away from each other. The phantom sensation of Graham's body made him feel warm all over.

"Thanks," he said.

"Anytime. Steak?"

"Steak."

NINE

GOING out to dinner with Graham was nothing like their lunch outing. For one thing, Graham drove, which made Jake feel a little bit like they were on a date with Jake in the awkward virgin role and Graham as the older, experienced suitor. They weren't on a date, of course, but Jake still had a tight ball of nerves in his stomach, as if he was liable to do the wrong thing at any moment and Graham would go haring back to Boston.

The awkwardness wasn't helped that even with the seat racked back all the way, Jake's knees were still in the vicinity of the glove compartment. They limited conversation on the way to the steakhouse to Jake's driving directions and small talk about Graham's room at the motel, which was apparently almost as big as the small apartment he lived in.

"We've got more space out here in the country," Jake said.

"It's nice. The city gets kind of claustrophobic sometimes. But there are perks to make up for it; museums and shows and stuff."

Jake thought he'd like to go to a museum with Graham. Or a baseball game. Or a movie. Or anything, really. They were almost at the restaurant when he decided he had nothing to lose by telling Graham the truth. Not about the fact that he'd mistaken him for a sex worker earlier in the day. That was still too mortifying to even acknowledge. But there was something else true that he could say. "Graham?"

"Yeah?"

"Take this left, and then it'll be on your right." Jake took a deep breath and steeled himself to say the rest. "I've had a really great day. Thank you."

Graham made the left turn, nosed the Civic into the half-full steakhouse parking lot and parked. He turned to Jake. "I'm really glad. And the day's not over yet." He winked again and got out of the car. Jake really didn't think he'd ever get used to the sheer adorableness-slash-sexiness of that minute gesture. He scrambled to get out and follow Graham to the entrance.

Graham held the door open for him and requested a table for two from the hostess behind the little podium at the front of the dark wood-paneled restaurant.

Jake had been to Singer's Steakhouse dozens of times, but it had never been like this. He had never felt like he was part of a couple before. And maybe he didn't have much to compare it to, and maybe this was how Graham was with all his friends, but it sure as hell *felt* like they were on a date. Was it all in his head, or did Graham feel it, too?

They were seated at a nice table in a quiet corner. After they each ordered a beer, Graham excused himself to use the bathroom, and Jake used his time by himself to freak out slightly.

If this felt like a date, then maybe it was a date. And if it was a date, then what did that mean? Did Graham like him? Was that why Graham had come all this way? If so, why hadn't he said something like, "Jake, I like you." Was Jake supposed to ask? He was so confused, and he didn't want to break the mood by asking something so potentially humiliating.

Because things had been so amazing. Just having Graham here and getting to know the person he'd been friends with for years all that much better was incredible. He wasn't that different in person from the way he was online, honestly. But now his friend had a voice to go with the name. In the future, whenever they chatted online, he'd be hearing Graham say the words in his smooth baritone with the slight twang. Graham had a face now, too. It had never mattered to Jake that he didn't know what his friend looked like. But he'd been able to learn new things by spending time with Graham in person, like the way he stuck his hands in his pockets when he was a little nervous or feeling shy, or the different smiles he had for different situations.

It was a lot. And he didn't want to ruin a good thing by asking the most childish question imaginable—*do you, like, like me?*

Yeah, he wouldn't say anything. He was going to have dinner with his friend and put any idea that this could be a romantic date out of his head entirely. He'd still be having the best birthday he'd ever had.

"Sorry that took so long," Graham said, plopping back down in his chair.

"No problem." Jake offered his friend a smile.

Graham smiled back. "So, your dimples. I never got to finish what I was saying earlier. They're pretty cute."

Well, fuck it.

"Graham, is this a date?"

Graham blinked. "Um. That depends."

"On what?"

"Look, maybe we should order first?"

Jake was starving, but he needed answers more than food. "No, please finish a thought for once today. What are we doing? Why did you come here today? I'm going crazy here, man. Please."

Graham shifted in his chair. "You're right. I'm sorry. I —I forget you aren't in my head sometimes. You seem to know me so well, but I know I keep a lot inside and it can be hard for me to get it out."

"Take as much time as you need. I don't want to make you uncomfortable. But I'm not sure exactly what's going on."

Their server chose that moment to show up, order pad at the ready. On autopilot, Jake asked for his usual order, a New York strip medium rare, loaded baked potato, and creamed spinach. Graham didn't hesitate before ordering the same, with a side of blue cheese for the steak. The second their server left, Jake stared Graham right in the eyes and said, "Talk to me."

Graham settled back in his chair, green eyes serious. "All right. I told you earlier today about Mitch. How it took me a long time to be ready to date again. It's been—wow, nearly six years—and for the first three I didn't date. At all. The grief group helped. No one in my life in Boston seemed to understand what I was going through. Losing him like that—someone I loved, someone I thought was going to be my future, and having him torn away in a second. No one understood what that was like, except in the group. Remember when I said you inspired to me to date again? Well, it's because I was damaged, but I had to get better if I wanted to be with someone as amazing as you."

Jake nodded, encouraging Graham to go on, even if some of what he was saying made no sense.

"But it didn't work. I'd go out with guys I met on an app, or through a friend, or at a bar, and it was okay, but something was always off. Eventually, I realized I was picking guys I knew were wrong for me because I was scared to let myself be with someone I could have a real future with. Someone like you."

"Like me?" Jake squeaked.

"I broke up with the last one, when all I wanted to do when I was out with him was get home so I could get online and talk to you." Graham huffed out a dry laugh. "But I didn't think you felt the same way. I didn't know how to bring it up without it getting weird. And then, a few days ago, you said you liked me, and we should meet —I saw it as a sign to just get over myself and come see if you felt the same way. And then I got here and you were so—"

Graham broke off at that, took a sip of his beer. Jake

was on tenterhooks waiting to see how Graham was going to finish that sentence, but since he'd talked more in the past several minutes than the entire day combined, he felt like he could give him a moment. When one minute turned into two, Jake had to break the silence.

"So geeky and awkward?" he said, half joking.

Graham frowned. His voice went hard. "No. So goddamn gorgeous. I started second guessing myself right away. Maybe you had a boyfriend that you never mentioned or I wasn't your type or —"

"Graham, stop. I'm—you're—you think I'm gorgeous?" Jake couldn't keep the patent disbelief out of his tone.

"Uh, yeah," Graham said, as if it was self-evident. "You're tall and you've got those shoulders, but then your waist, I could just—" He made a hand motion Jake couldn't quite interpret. "—and your smile, it's like sun breaking through the clouds with those dimples and your eyes. And your hands—um. They're really. Well. I just. Yeah. You're gorgeous and I don't know what's the matter with the guys of Apple Vale if you aren't getting hit on every day of the week, but I'm really attracted to you and I'm going to stop talking now."

"Wow." That was a lot to absorb. Not that Jake thought Graham was lying or putting him on, but it was going to take a minute for any of that to sink into his brain.

Graham took another sip of his beer, and a moment later two giant platters of food appeared on their table. Jake was too preoccupied to taste his food as he started eating, but then he noticed Graham wasn't eating at all.

"Are you okay?"

"Sure. It would be nice to know what you're thinking about all of that, I guess," Graham said a trifle miserably.

"Oh! God. I'm so sorry." Jake put down his knife and fork, swiped his napkin over his mouth. "I'm still kind of getting used to...everything. Thank you for telling me, really." He took a deep breath. "And what you said, about thinking I didn't feel the same way. Yeah. Same. I've had feelings for you for a while, but I didn't know how to tell you. And then you showed up here, out of the blue, and you're, like, totally my type, by the way. I'm pretty sure tall, handsome, and incredibly nice is everyone's type."

Graham straight up laughed at that. Jake's heart quivered happily at the sound. "I didn't know what to do, either."

"So, to be clear, we both had feelings for each other before today," Graham said.

"And we're both attracted to each other," Jake added.

"And we're eating dinner alone together. I think this can officially be called a date."

"Cool," Jake said calmly, even though his stomach was a mass of butterflies at having been proven right in the most spectacular fashion possible.

Graham's smile was so wide his eye crinkles had crinkles. "Cool," he repeated. And together they dug into their meals with relish.

TEN

AFTER DECIDING they were officially on a date, time sped up. They talked and laughed and both polished their plates clean. Jake had two beers, but Graham stuck to one, since he was driving. His face had shuttered slightly when ordering another round came up, and Jake knew that Graham was thinking about Mitch. But then Graham seemed to remember that Jake knew the story, and he relaxed. No more explanations were necessary.

Jake loved feeling that he and Graham were getting closer. And everything was fine when he focused on the fact that Graham liked being with him, that they were on the same page about having more-than-friendly feelings for each other.

But what made his leg jiggle nervously under the table was thinking about the other part. The part where Graham said he was—quote, gorgeous. The part where he'd admitted to Graham he was attracted to him. Which had to be obvious, but still, it was out there.

He tried telling himself that being on a date and

having stated their mutual physical attraction didn't mean that anything was going to happen. But it didn't mean nothing was going to happen either. And he thought Graham deserved to know something before they got too far down the road of not-nothing.

"This is my new favorite restaurant," Graham announced as he leaned back in his chair, replete. "That creamed spinach was amazing."

"Yeah, who knew all it took was three different kinds of dairy products to make spinach delicious?" Jake said.

Graham laughed. Jake decided that making Graham laugh was his new favorite thing. "I'll bet you have room for dessert, though, Stretch?" Graham said speculatively.

Now that Jake knew Graham wasn't making fun of him, he kind of liked the nickname. It meant they were close enough for nicknames. He wondered what his nickname for Graham could be.

Mr. Right seemed too on the nose.

Jake dragged his mind back to the conversation at hand. "Dessert, yes, always."

"That's what I thought." Graham motioned to their server, who'd been hovering semi- obviously in the corner, but instead of coming to their table, she disappeared into the back, then came out again with an entire cheesecake topped high with strawberries and whipped cream and about a thousand candles, which she carried over carefully and placed on the table between them.

Graham started singing the birthday song and Jake didn't know what was more surprising—the fact that he'd arranged all of this somehow, or that he sounded good singing the birthday song.

Graham's singing voice was improbably clear and strong and his country twang came out even more. How on earth was Jake lucky enough to be on a date with a guy who sounded sexy singing "Happy Birthday to You?"

The last notes of the song died away and Graham grinned excitedly, his face lit up by the glow of all those birthday candles. "Make a wish, Jake!"

Jake closed his eyes for a moment. He'd made a wish this morning, from a place of loneliness, a place of dissatisfaction. His wish, for something to change, had come true. He was nervous to make another one. Maybe he'd used up his share of birthday wish mojo and this one wouldn't come true. On the other hand, now he had definitive proof that birthday wishes could come true. In that case, he sort of had to go for it, didn't he?

He opened his eyes, made his wish, and blew out the candles with one great whoosh of air.

Graham whooped and hollered and clapped, and Jake couldn't even be embarrassed because Graham looked so happy.

"This is amazing. I love cheesecake."

"I know."

"And your voice—I didn't know you could sing."

Graham looked down bashfully. "I'm okay. Sometimes I sing with my friend's band. Just open mics, stuff like that."

Another clue that Graham was completely out of Jake's league.

"Thank you for doing this. You didn't have to."

"I did, though. I wanted your birthday to be one to remember."

"I could never forget this birthday," Jake promised. "I hope you aren't expecting me to eat this entire cake, though, because I might die."

"No, let's start with a piece. You can take the rest home."

"I'll bring a piece to Nana tomorrow. She's an even bigger cheesecake freak than me."

"But not as big as me, probably," Graham said, cutting himself a massive wedge. "What? This is a special occasion," he said when he caught sight of Jake's raised eyebrows.

"My birthday is a special occasion for you? By what rules?"

"While I am happy to be celebrating your birthday, I meant it's a special occasion because, well, it's our first date."

Jake was an ass, making everything about him. "Oh. That's right." Not only was this their first date, but according to Graham, he hadn't been on any dates in nearly a year. This was kind of a big deal. His leg started jiggling again.

Graham served him a slightly less massive slice of cake, and the first bite helped his nerves. The second and third bites did, too. Thusly fortified with sugar, he had to just say it.

"Graham, I have to tell you something."

"This is the best cheesecake you've ever had? Seriously, this place is a find. I have yet to locate decent cheesecake in Boston. Good ice cream, yes. I'll have to take you to my favorite place sometime. Do you like nuts in your ice cream?"

"Well, yes, but it's not about that. It's just something I think you should know, before...later."

"I'm listening." Graham licked his fork and put it down.

Jake fought against the distraction of Graham's tongue and tried to put his thoughts into words. "I think you know I don't have much experience dating." Jake's perpetual single status had come up once or twice in their online chats. Graham had always been warmly supportive that he'd find someone when he was ready.

Instead of nodding, Graham winced. "Yeah, about that."

"Huh?"

"I feel kind of bad, but whenever you'd bring that up, I was always secretly glad that you weren't seeing anyone. It was totally selfish of me. Maybe I should have encouraged you to go out more or something."

"No, that's not on you," Jake said. "Where I live there's not a huge queer dating scene. Or if there is, I don't know about it. I got deep into a comfort zone, and I didn't want to get out of it. That's on me. Besides, I was crushing on you too hard to become interested in anyone else, even if there was anyone else to be interested in."

"So I'm not a consolation prize?" Graham said, trying to soften the question with a smile.

"No, of course not. I wouldn't even bring this up, but I want to make it clear that my lack of experience with dating extends, um, kind of far. Like, all the way, so to speak."

Graham looked confused.

"As in," Jake tried not to blush, "I've never gone...all

the way." It sounded juvenile to put it like that, but Jake couldn't force himself to say the word virgin.

"Oh." Graham's confusion melted away, replaced with something Jake hoped wasn't pity. "Thanks for telling me." He looked at the half-eaten slice of cheese-cake on his plate and then up again. "Does this mean you aren't interested in that? Which is totally okay."

"No! That's not what I meant. I'm very much interested in that. With you."

"Yeah?" Graham looked at him, his lids half-lowered, green eyes framed by golden eyelashes like jade surrounded by gilt.

Jake swallowed heavily. "Yeah."

"Okay." Graham reached across the table, holding his hand palm up. It took Jake a beat to figure out that he wanted Jake to meet him halfway. He extended his own hand and placed it in Graham's. It was apparently the right thing to do because Graham squeezed his hand reas-suringly. "We'll just go slow."

"Slow, right." Jake liked the way his hand felt in Graham's. His was a little bigger, but Graham's was firm and strong. He knew that hand would feel incredible on other parts of his body. Suddenly, the simple touch made him feel hot all over, as if he'd stepped into the blazing heat of a summer's day, or too close to a roaring fireplace. "Slow is good. But maybe we could get started, oh, fairly quickly?"

Graham grinned toothily. "I'm on board with that." He withdrew his hand, and Jake would have been disap-pointed, but he used it to get their server back over to request a box for the cake.

"What about the check?" Jake asked when they had most of a cheesecake safely ensconced in a brown box. "I've got my gift card."

"Save it to take Nana out. It's all taken care of," Graham said lightly.

"I can't let you—"

"It's done. You can buy next time."

Next time. Jake floated back to the car on the promise of next time, and ice cream, and moving slow as fast as possible.

ELEVEN

THEY GOT INTO THE CIVIC, Jake folding into an origami version of himself to fit in the front seat, cake box balanced on his lap. Graham looked over, did something complicated with his mouth, then gently took the cake box off Jake's lap and set it in the backseat. He stuck the key in the ignition but didn't turn the car on. Instead, he shifted to face Jake.

"You said you've never...but there are things you have done, right?"

"Uh. Sure."

"Could you be more specific?"

"Why?"

"I really want to kiss you, but I've been building it up in my mind all day. Or probably longer, to be honest. But I'm psyching myself out worrying that maybe you haven't kissed anyone, and I'd be your first kiss and that puts all kinds of pressure on a guy so I figured I'd ask instead of going around in circles in the old noggin."

Jake had to smile at how adorably flustered Graham was getting. "Noggin?"

"Whatever. Just—have you?"

"Have I kissed anyone?"

"Yes," Graham ground out, cheeks reddening.

Jake liked being able to wind him up, but it was a fair question. "Yes. I kissed a few guys in high school. There may have been some over-the-clothes touching. But again, Apple Vale High wasn't a really safe place to be out and proud, so my opportunities were limited. I told myself college would be different, but then my dad got sick. My priorities changed. And, as you know, I never made it out of Apple Vale."

"Okay. Wow. So that's it?"

Jake didn't know what to make of Graham's tight features. "Yeah. Sorry."

"Don't apologize, Jake. I'm just." He rubbed his hands on his denim-clad thighs nervously. "It's been a while for me, too. But a perfectionist about some things. When I'm not sure I'm going to do something perfectly, I talk myself out of doing it at all."

"Is kissing me something you're talking yourself out of? Because I would very much like it if you'd talk yourself back into it."

"Yeah?" Graham said, then he bit his lip and Jake had to control himself in order not to visibly react.

"And also remember, I don't have a lot to compare it to. Not to mention I highly doubt anyone with a—" Jake broke off. He felt kind of bad about how baldly he had been about to objectify his friend-slash-date.

Graham cocked his head. "What?"

"Just, your mouth looks like it was made for kissing, that's all," Jake mumbled, tipping his head forward in the hopes his hair would shield his burning cheeks from Graham's gaze.

"Oh yeah? Well, yours does, too. I've been wanting to taste that pouty bottom of lip of yours since you opened the door this morning."

Jake pushed away the reminder of that first encounter. "Well, you can."

Graham put his hand on Jake's knee, using his other hand to brush Jake's hair back from his face, his palm lingering on Jake's jaw. Jake swallowed. They weren't very far apart in the little car, but it still felt like an absurdly long journey as they leaned forward, slowly erasing the distance between them like two lovers in a romantic comedy.

It wasn't perfect; they bumped noses before their mouths connected, Graham's lips felt dry against Jake's, or maybe it was his own lips that were dry, but then Graham opened his mouth a little, and Jake felt a tongue pressing at the seam of his lips. He opened up, trying to remember how to do this.

Graham's tongue touched his and it was like he'd activated a direct line to Jake's dick, because he was suddenly half hard. He moaned into Graham's mouth and the hand that was on Jake's knee tightened almost painfully. Graham kissed him harder, the hand on his neck keeping him close. Jake didn't know what to do with his own hands. He knocked one into the gear shift trying to find Graham's knee, then settled for putting one hand on Graham's shoulder. His firm, masculine shoulder. Speculating about what Graham looked like without a shirt on had him all the way hard in seconds.

He broke off the kiss with a gasp. Maybe Graham had a point with slow. He was ready to blow in his jeans after two minutes of kissing and while he knew Graham wouldn't give him a hard time about it, there were limits to his tolerance for mortification.

"Okay?" Graham asked, voice like gravel.

"So okay," Jake said. He sounded breathy to his own ears, and he actually felt a little lightheaded. He sucked in a breath, trying to get himself under control.

"But?"

"But I'm—you're. We're *kissing*," Jake said in wonder.

"Yeah, we are," Graham agreed, as if it was the best thing ever.

"I so didn't expect this to happen today," Jake said, head still spinning.

Graham sat back in his seat at that, which made Jake wish he hadn't said anything. They were still touching, but there was space between them now. Jake didn't want to stop, but he didn't know how to go on, either.

"I know," Graham said. "I feel like today's been incredible but also not really real, you know?"

Considering Graham was Jake's fantasy come to life, he did know. "Yeah."

"I mean, I had all these ideas. I'd meet you and we'd hit it off, and maybe, if I was lucky, you'd want to see if we could...be together, somehow. But—"

Jake already didn't like where Graham was going with that but. "We did hit it off," he said quickly.

"I know. But you know what I learned today? You

took me on the Jake Crane tour of Apple Vale and I got to see this whole amazing life you have. You have your family and your job and your volunteer work and you have a house where you could have a dog."

"You think my life is amazing?"

"You make so many people's lives better, Jake, just by being in theirs."

"Well, what about you? You're a teacher. You have friends, a life in Boston. You do open mics. And you make my life better, Graham."

"I know," Graham said sadly. "I guess I figured I'd be rescuing you from suburbia and you'd want to...I don't know, come back to Boston with me?"

"Come back with you? Like, *move* there?"

Graham wasn't looking at him. He let out a joyless laugh. "It was a stupid idea. I don't know what I was thinking."

Jake hadn't been thinking much beyond *Graham. Beautiful. Date. Kissing. Sex?* But the reality that they lived over four hours apart was bringing him down to earth fast. "Shit."

"It's not like it's impossible—long distance, I mean," Graham said, "if you'd want to try."

Jake said nothing. He knew it was crazy to want to move to a huge city in a different state after a steak and a two-minute make-out session, but he couldn't imagine not having Graham in his life in a tangible way now that he'd finally met him. But he'd spent so long in the same place. Seeing his home through Graham's eyes today, he could see what he was saying. Who would check on Nana and recruit volunteers for the animal shelter and he'd already accepted the job at the hospital and—

Graham's turning the key in the ignition startled him out of his thoughts. "I'll take you home," he said. "We should get that cake in the fridge."

"Okay." Jake didn't have any answers. He could only hope that his birthday cheesecake wouldn't be the only thing he'd get to keep from today.

TWELVE

GRAHAM SEEMED to remember the way back, even though it was past sundown. Jake only had to remind him once about a turn and then suddenly they were on Jake's street. He hadn't gotten any closer to figuring out what to do, how to get them back to the easy intimacy of their date, when Graham's face had been lit up by the glow of birthday candles and Jake had felt an answering glow in his chest.

His house loomed, windows dark, the porch light the only illumination. Beauty was still parked in the driveway. Graham pulled the Civic to a stop in front. Jake's stomach sank when he realized Graham hadn't turned the engine off. So, this was it? He was being dropped off like a ten-year-old after a birthday party?

How had things gotten so far off track? Yeah, they had some real-life issues to work out now that they'd gone from virtual friends to two flesh-and-blood people who wanted more than a virtual relationship. But they could figure it out, couldn't they?

"Look—" he started just as Graham said, "Jake—"

"You go first," they said at the same time.

Jake smiled, and Graham smiled back shyly. They were on the same page about so many things; he had to believe he wouldn't lose Graham so soon after getting him.

"I really like you," Graham said quietly. "And this is a big deal for both of us. I meant what I said about slow. I think if we take this slow, we can avoid...mistakes."

Jake frowned. He agreed this was a big deal. But what did Graham mean by mistakes? "You mean like when you overthink your messages to me and google memes and probably retype them ten times until they're perfect? Graham, life isn't a chat box. You can't keep me waiting on your bouncing bubbles forever."

Graham put his hands on the steering wheel and gripped it tight. "You should put the cheesecake in the fridge," he said gruffly.

"Oh." Jake floundered. He didn't know how to fix this. It was like when he'd messaged Graham that last time and heard nothing for two days. He'd thought he'd done something wrong and didn't know what to do. And now he had Graham right in front of him and the feeling was that times ten. "Do you want to come in?"

Graham sighed. "Sorry. I've got a long drive tomorrow. I'm going to get some sleep."

Jake blinked. It was barely nine. The sensation of being rejected was new, but he understood it for what it was. He reached to the backseat and lifted the cake box, opened the door, and levered himself out of the car.

"Breakfast?" he asked, too sad to worry about seeming desperate.

"Maybe. Yeah. I'll text you."

"Okay. Thanks for dinner, Graham."

"Happy birthday, Jake."

It was so final. So impersonal, after everything they'd shared with each other. Jake slammed the car door a little harder than necessary. He watched as Graham steered the Civic down the street until he turned on the next block and out of view.

He looked down at the brown box in his hands and smiled wryly. At least he had almost an entire cheesecake to drown his sorrows with. He let himself into the house. It was dark and quiet; his mom must not have come home yet. Of course, his forty-eight-year-old mother had a better social life than her twenty-four-year-old son.

Jake switched on the light in the kitchen. He flipped open the lid of the box, not because he was hungry but to remind himself that Graham had arranged this for him—thought about him and made something special happen just because it was his birthday and Graham liked him and wanted to. They were turning out to be kind of terrible at this, but at least he had the evidence of Graham's feelings right here. He looked down at the cake. The strawberry sauce had slid off the side, staining the cheesecake underneath a garish red. The depressions on the surface where the candles had been were pooled with sticky red sauce and melted whipped cream. It was a mess. Jake closed the lid quickly. No need to take the cake-as-relationship metaphor too far.

He sighed and shoved the box into the fridge. What

now? Normally when he felt down, he'd get on his computer and see if Graham was around, but he knew all he'd find if he went online were unanswered birthday messages and Chip. He shut his eyes against the reality of Chip. Okay, so that was out. Maybe he should head to bed. He and Graham would both get some sleep, and things would be better in the morning. Graham would text him and—

Shit. Graham wouldn't text him. He didn't have his number. They'd never exchanged actual telephone numbers, preferring to use the app. No big deal. He'd check his messages in the morning.

Jake's shoulders rounded over as he retraced his steps, flicking the kitchen light off on his way to the stairs. He caught sight of himself in the hallway mirror. He'd forgotten he was wearing his dad's jacket. With all his might, he wished his dad was here to tell him what do to, to tell him things were going to be okay. He missed him so much.

He sat down on the first step, unable to muster the energy to go all the way upstairs. His dad had always been there for him, and that had been the hardest thing about his passing—James Crane had understood that his being sick meant he would no longer be there for his son. His dad told him as much when it became apparent the cancer was progressing faster than any treatment could stem. "I'm going to miss out on a lot of things," his dad had said. "I hate like hell I won't be there when you graduate college or get your first real job or get married. I wish I could stop this from happening. Just remember—you won't be alone, even if I'm not there."

Jake had felt alone, though. He'd used the grief from his dad's death to insulate himself from taking risks, but it had also insulated him from making connections. And now he had made a connection with a guy he really cared about. A hot guy, even. And he didn't know what to do.

"What should I do, Dad?" he asked the empty house.

There was no answer.

There was no answer because the house was fucking empty. He was literally alone. Graham had gone. His mom was off living her life. Nana was surrounded by friends at The Vale. He didn't even have a dog to commiserate with. This was ridiculous.

This morning he'd wished for something to change, and Graham had shown up like a miracle, but here, alone in the dark on his birthday, Jake finally got it. He couldn't always be staring at a screen, waiting for Graham's dots to resolve into words. He couldn't keep living in the house he'd lived in for twenty-four years, eating the same pancakes, doing the same chores, seeing the same people over and over for infinity. He had to make the change. Him, Jake Crane, son of James and Liv Crane, grandson of Jonathan and Elizabeth Crane. He was a third generation Apple Vale resident, but that didn't mean he had to stay here forever.

If he wanted something to change, he'd have to do it himself.

THIRTEEN

THE SHADOW BROOK Motel was on the outskirts of town, past the animal shelter, almost to Atkins Farm, which used to be a real working dairy farm and was now a trendily rustic events venue. On the drive over, Jake put aside his anxiety about what he was going to say to Graham in favor of anxiety about how to figure out Graham's room number. Going in and asking at the front desk seemed potentially problematic. Weren't there rules against telling random people what rooms customers were in?

He pulled into the motel, a single-story L-shaped building set back from the highway. Most of the parking spaces in front of the two-dozen rooms were full. Jake scanned the vehicles and noticed a lot of out-of-state plates, a few New York ones, including a Volvo wagon the same model as his mom's. Graham's car, Massachusetts plates and all, was parked in the very last spot in front of the very last room. It was possible Graham had parked at the end because it was the only spot he could get, but then he saw movement in the window directly in front of the Civic—a flash of sandy brown hair as Graham snapped the curtains shut against the glare of Jake's headlights. Jake found a space in the center of the row, killed the engine, and took a few calming breaths.

He could do this. Even if he failed spectacularly, at least he would know he tried. Besides, Graham was worth risking almost anything.

That didn't mean taking the plunge wasn't terrifying. He got out of the truck slowly, carefully locking it up. He forced himself to put one foot in front of the other until he got to the room he'd seen Graham inside. Room 24. Huh. He was twenty-four today. Maybe it was a sign. He gathered all his courage and knocked. A short wait, then he heard Graham shuffling on the other side of the door.

"Graham? It's Jake."

The door flew open. Graham stood there, wearing the same jeans and shirt, but barefoot. Jake's gaze lingered slightly on his first glimpse of Graham's feet. He'd never thought of feet as particularly sexy, but of course Graham's were. He'd always privately despaired of his own prehensile-length digits. Graham's feet were normally proportioned with a dusting of blond hair on the toes.

He sighed, half in admiration, half in envy, and lifted his gaze. Graham was looking at him with a strange expression.

"I'm sorry to just show up, but to be fair, you pulled the unannounced entrance card first, so here I am."

"Here you are," Graham agreed.

"I'd like to come in and talk. And by talk, I mean tell

you some things. Hopefully get your response, but if you need more time to process, I'll wait. I'll wait as long as it takes. I'm sorry about what I said earlier. I shouldn't have made it seem like I minded you taking your time with things. I don't. I'd wait for you forever, probably, but I'm hoping I won't have to." Jake wasn't sure how his speech was coming off, but Graham wasn't shutting the door in his face, so that was a win.

After a pause, Graham said, "Then you better come in." He stepped back to let Jake through before shutting the door behind him. The room held just a bed, a TV, a desk, and single chair, but it was clean and not horribly ugly. The ceiling was low, though. Jake already felt like a giant, so he sat on the chair. Graham took the edge of the bed.

Graham said nothing, so Jake figured he was waiting for Jake to get the point. "I was sitting alone in the house I've lived in all my life in the dark on my birthday and I realized some things."

Graham's nod seemed to mean he wanted him to go on, even though his body language was reserved, as if he was waiting to hear what Jake said before he gave anything away. Well, fine, Jake was prepared to make a fool of himself if that's what it took.

"First, I want your cell number." He got out his phone and poised his fingers over the screen. "Please?"

The smile that appeared on Graham's lips was tiny, but it was there. He reeled off ten digits and Jake typed them in, then sent the number a text. Graham's phone rattled on the desktop behind him. "Now you have mine."

"You're very organized," Graham said. There might have been the hint of amusement in his voice.

"Occasionally." The rush Jake got from accomplishing that small feat gave him the courage to say his next piece. "Second, you told me today that not loving doesn't stop you from getting hurt. And the truth is, I've been in pain for a long time. I thought it was just since my dad died, but really it started before that, before he got sick even, when I realized I was gay, and didn't know how that was going to work living in a small town. I was scared to be myself. I was scared people wouldn't like me if I didn't conform to their expectations of me. Losing Dad was just another excuse to cut myself off from a lot of the world."

He ran a hand through his hair, nervous to say the next part, but Graham sat calmly, hands resting lightly on his knees. He looked effortlessly handsome, but also a little melancholy. Jake was still not used to how attractive he found Graham, and yet what was more compelling was that air of sadness. Jake wanted to help give Graham a reason to leave the sadness by the wayside. He forged on.

"Alone got to be a habit, but I don't want to be alone anymore. The last three years I've known you, I haven't been alone when I was talking with you. And I'm not willing to give up on this just because we live in different states. Whatever dating long distance looks like, we'll figure it out. I want to, anyway, and I hope you do, too. I want to be with you, Graham."

Jake figured it would take Graham time to figure out how to respond to that, but he wasn't done with his list, so he kept going. Graham would have his turn soon.

"Third. I'm moving out of my mom's house. I don't know where to yet, but it's time. My mom deserves some privacy, and I need to be on my own. Nana gave me the push I needed today, but I've known I've needed to do it for a while."

Graham raised his eyebrows at that, but still said nothing, so Jake moved on to his fourth and final point. "Last thing. I want to kiss you again. Like a lot. Maybe lying down. Okay, that's it."

In the silence that followed Jake felt a confusing mixture of pride at having said what he came there to say, hope that while Graham had said nothing positive in response, he hadn't shut him down, either, and fear that by being too honest he might scare Graham away for good. He tried to focus on the first two emotions and waited.

FOURTEEN

GRAHAM HADN'T MOVED, except to rub his hands on the top of his thighs.

Jake was starting to worry that he'd broken Graham permanently, but then he started speaking in a halting, low tone. "Jake, you might have noticed I tend to second guess myself. I second guessed myself right out of your arms earlier and I've been beating myself up about it ever since. You just said a lot of brave stuff, and I appreciate you telling me all of that. But the thing I appreciate the most is that you came here at all, that you weren't willing to let me punk out and run away, when being with you is the only thing I've wanted for so long."

All of that sounded incredible to Jake, but he had to give Graham space to finish. He tamped down on the elation that wanted to erupt in his chest while Graham went on.

"Like you, I've been in pain for a long time. It's not the same, but since Mitch passed, I've spent a lot of time punishing myself, and scared, and using missing him to put off certain aspects of my life. One thing I know for sure is we both deserve a chance to have something good, to give this thing between us a chance. And I don't know what it looks like, either, but we're pretty smart; we'll figure it out."

That was good enough for Jake. He wanted to get started right away, even though he had no idea what the first step was. But Graham went on, "I think if you're ready to move out, you should. I'll help you move if you want."

"Thank you."

"As for the last thing—the kissing thing." Graham smiled, a ray of light in the dim room. "I think that can be arranged. I mean, there's a bed right here. Perfect for lying down kissing."

"That's true."

"So what do you say? Are we doing this? Are we actually going to let ourselves be happy?"

"I think so," Jake said. "I think being with you is going to make me really happy, Graham."

"Me, too."

They stared at each other wearing equally dopey grins until Jake cracked and launched himself at Graham, sprawling them both backward on the bed. Graham laughed and retaliated by tickling Jake's side under his jacket, until suddenly they were rolling around, half wrestling, half tickle fighting, laughing like little boys. Somewhere in there, Jake shed his jacket and kicked off his sneakers. Graham's hair was mussed, and he looked young and happy. Jake's heart expanded in his chest until it almost hurt with joy.

He dipped his head down and caught Graham's lips with his. He kissed him soft and light. Graham deepened the kiss on a groan, and then they were doing a new type of wrestling, hands skimming beneath each other's shirts to the skin underneath, tentative touches over denim. The first time Graham's hand found Jake's ass and squeezed, Jake had to bite down on his lip to keep from coming right there and then.

"Is this okay? Do you want to stop? We can just kiss," Graham said, tilting his forehead to rest it on Jake's, their hands stilling between them.

"This is good. Um. I'm okay with going a little farther," Jake said.

"Why don't you start, and I'll follow your lead?"

Jake appreciated Graham letting him set the boundaries of what he was comfortable with. But he was past his earlier hesitance. He trusted Graham and yeah, he was nervous, because while touching and being touched by Graham felt wonderful, it was still new. But he wasn't scared. He knew what he wanted.

He tugged his shirt over his head, unbuttoned his fly but left his jean on. Graham scanned his chest, eyes wide. Jake didn't exactly work out with any regularity, but he got exercise. The animal shelter always seemed to have boxes to lift and carry, fifty-pound bags of dog and cat food to move around. He ran the dogs in the yard. His work at the nursing home was more geared toward talk therapy, but Nana always seemed to need something heavy moved, and then the other residents would ask her grandson to spare a hand to move a piece of furniture around their small apartments. Consequently, he had flat abs and defined pecs.

Graham eyed him, tongue peeking out of his mouth. Damn. Jake would never be able to decide which of Graham's mannerisms was the sexiest. Was it the wink? The lip biting? Or maybe it was the little lip lick he was doing right now as he perused Jake's naked chest.

"Like I said, gorgeous," Graham said. He unbuttoned his own shirt, shrugged it off. He didn't have an undershirt on and Jake was treated to an expanse of creamy skin, dark pink nipples, freckles that tempted him to lean over and lick. But he didn't touch, just watched as Graham unzipped his jeans to what looked like white briefs underneath. Jake's dick twitched as a new piece of information entered his mental file under Graham's name. He'd found white briefs sexy ever since his adolescent sexual awakening had involved an obsession with a certain Calvin Klein ad.

"You're pretty gorgeous yourself. Can I—" He didn't know how to finish the sentence, because there were so very many things he wanted to do.

"You can do anything you want," Graham said, low and sexy.

Jake took him at his word, lowered his head and licked a stripe over Graham's nipples, one after the other. They beaded up instantly, and when he did it a second time, he tongued the nubs experimentally. Graham sucked in a breath through his teeth and Jake's cock throbbed sympathetically.

He spent a little longer exploring what sounds he

could make Graham utter, then looked up through his bangs. Graham's head was thrown back, the line of his neck an erotic arch that had Jake licking and nipping his way to his chin. They were chest to chest now, and the press of Graham's skin against his was heaven on earth. Graham moved closer and suddenly their groins pushed together, open flies rubbing against each other, the hard line of Graham's cock unmistakable as it slotted up against Jake's.

"Fuck," Graham said, slipping his hands underneath the jeans to lay his hands firmly on Jake's ass. "You feel so good."

Jake considered that to be an enormous understatement. "Yeah, that feels good."

From there, it seemed natural as anything to keep kissing and rutting against each other, Graham's hands working Jake's ass, Jake keeping the rhythm going with his palms planted on either side of Graham's shoulders. He wanted everything at once, but this felt too good to stop. Graham was making these sweet, choked moans every time Jake rolled his hips a certain way, so he kept doing it until Graham said, "Wait." Jake stopped instantly and looked down at Graham's flushed face.

"Let's not ruin our jeans, okay?" Graham said. He let go of Jake long enough to wriggle out of his pants. Jake followed suit. He supposed Graham had a point—neither of them had tons of extra clothes on hand. He took off his socks, then took a deep breath for courage and slipped out of his boxers, too. Graham was indeed wearing white briefs, which Jake took a moment to appreciate while Graham was turned away tossing his jeans onto the chair.

When he looked back to see Jake fully naked, he froze. "Jake. Fuck. You're...."

Jake looked down at himself. Was there something wrong with his dick? Were his balls a weird shape? He'd seen his share of porn, but everyone knew porn wasn't exactly reality central. "Is this okay?" he asked hesitantly. "You look amazing, by the way." Graham's body was lean but a little soft, so much beautiful milky skin to pore over, to worship.

"Thanks. And yeah, it's okay. Can I?" Graham pulled at the waistband of his underwear.

"Sure, of course." This was it. He was going to see his first erect penis in person. And it was Graham's. How was this his life?

"You look amazing, too," Graham said as he stripped off the briefs. "And I didn't mean to make you uncomfortable. You're just really hung."

Jake felt his cheeks warm up. Yeah. He'd kind of always suspected maybe he had a little more going on in the size area than other guys, but he'd had nothing to compare it to. Besides porn. Which wasn't real. So. "Is that okay?"

"I think I can work with it," Graham said lightly. He laid back on the bed, inviting Jake to look. He didn't reject the invitation, gaze dropping to Graham's navel, which was being brushed by the tip of Graham's erection, lying flat and stiff on the trail of dark blond hairs leading to the thatch of neatly trimmed brown curls at the base of his cock. His balls lay tight underneath. Jake's mouth watered at the sight of them.

He was naked. With Graham. Holy fuck.

He let out an involuntary giggle and clapped a hand over his mouth as if he could belatedly hold it inside.

"What?" Graham began stroking his cock lazily, blowing Jake's mind for the umpteenth time that night.

"Sorry, I'm such a dork. It's just. You're super fucking hot and incredibly nice and I've never felt this way about anyone, and I guess I can't believe this is happening."

Graham let go of his cock and motioned to Jake. "Come here."

Jake shuffled up the bed, wondering for a second about the cleanliness of the comforter they were lying on. "This is weird, but could we get on the sheets?"

"Sure." Graham didn't even act like it was a strange request, simply shifted and kicked the comforter down the bed, peeled back the top sheet and resettled onto the slightly scratchy white motel bottom sheet. Jake positioned himself next to Graham's body, their hips touching. There was only one light on, on the table behind Graham; it gave him a golden aura that seemed fitting.

"Can I touch you?" Graham asked.

"Of course," Jake said.

Graham licked his lips, making them shiny. "I meant, specifically, can I touch your dick?"

"Specifically, yes, please."

Graham reached over, his beautiful, capable hand wrapping around Jake's cock, the other hand reaching lower to cup his balls, tugging them a little. "Okay?"

Jake thought it was a little unfair of Graham to expect him to make words while getting jerked off by his best friend, but he made an effort. "Good. Fuck."

Graham kept stroking, slow and sure, and moved his

other hand from Jake's balls to the space behind them, working his fingers against the tender flesh of his perineum. Jake widened his legs instinctively, and Graham wriggled farther back, the pad of his index finger brushing against Jake's asshole. He jumped a little, the sensation of being touched there an electric shock that had him bucking up into Graham's hand. Graham increased his pace, jerking Jake faster, not penetrating him with his finger, just pressing firmly.

"Kiss me," Graham said.

Jake realized he'd been lying there, letting Graham work him while he did nothing to contribute, but at Graham's sweet order he went into action, kissing Graham open-mouthed, getting one of his hands on Graham's dick. It was hot and silky smooth and felt different from his own cock, shorter but thicker, quite girthy in fact. Graham groaned into the kiss when Jake's thumb flicked over the head, so he did that again. He was so distracted by the sounds Graham was making, the overwhelming need to come suddenly blindsided him.

"Fuck, Graham, I'm going to—"

"Yeah, do it, come on," Graham panted. "Come, Jake." Then he pressed even harder on Jake's hole and pumped his cock and Jake lost his grip on Graham as his orgasm roared through him, a guttural moan wrenching from the depths of his chest. A hot flood of come coated Graham's hand and Jake's cock as Graham stroked him through it. Graham kissed him again, sweet and long, while he twitched through the last of the orgasm. He vaguely registered Graham's moans as he finished himself off. Jake looked down and saw Graham spilling into the hand that Jake had already covered with come. In a day of firsts, that was it—the hottest thing he'd experienced yet.

"Damn. Fuck. Graham." Those were all the words he was capable of producing.

Graham seemed to know what he meant. "Yeah?"

"Yeah." They kissed again, and then the combination of sweaty and sticky stopped being sexy. How long they were supposed to lay there before cleaning up?

Like the mind reader he was sometimes, Graham reached over to the nightstand and pulled out a handful of rough motel tissues from a slim box, offering them to Jake. He took them and mopped up the mess on his dick and pubes as best he could while Graham did the same with another handful.

"You want to take a shower?" Graham asked.

"In a minute." He marveled at how relaxed he felt, muscles pleasantly spent. "Thank you."

Graham turned on his side, casually, devastatingly handsome. He smiled with his eyes and took Jake's hand, lacing their fingers together. "Happy birthday, Jake." Then he raised their joined hands and kissed the back of Jake's. His smile dropped and he said seriously, "I'm yours, you know."

Jake's heart caught in his throat. "My what?"

"Your birthday present, I guess." Graham laughed softly. "But you're the true gift. Just being here with you. Being close with you. You letting me in. Giving me another chance. And I'm just—I don't know—I feel like I'm yours. Not like an ownership thing. But like...a privilege. It's a privilege to be with you this way."

Goosebumps formed on his arms as Graham spoke.

He knew everything from this moment would be seared into his memory forever. Graham being his. Him being Graham's. He'd remember this forever because it was the moment he knew with a thousand percent certainty he was in love.

FIFTEEN

NOW THAT JAKE knew he was in love, everything was suddenly...more. More intense, more beautiful. More terrifying.

He wanted to enjoy this time, cuddling with a naked Graham, his skin still hot and sensitive from what they'd done together, but his mind was racing with questions. If he felt this way, did Graham love him, too? Was it too soon to say anything? Was he supposed to just go home after this?

The last question, at least, was answered when Graham traced his fingers over Jake's collarbone and asked, "Would you like to spend the night?"

Jake looked into the eyes of the man he was in love with. They even looked greener after his realization. "Would you like me to?"

"Very much."

"Then I will."

Jake wanted to be cool about his first adult sleepover, but his mind filled with a type of insecurity he wished he'd been able to get over when he left his teenage years. He worried about everything from how he was going to brush his teeth to what would happen when they got into bed. Was Graham a cuddler? Was *he* a cuddler? He hadn't shared a bed with anyone since Cocoa.

But Graham made it easy on him. He slid off the bed, pulled on his briefs, rummaged around in his bag. "I don't have an extra toothbrush, but you can use my toothpaste." He held out a tube of Crest and motioned to the bathroom. Jake awkwardly grabbed his clothes from their various piles on the floor, took the tube and tried to not feel self-conscious about his bare ass on display as he disappeared into the bathroom as quickly as possible.

He splashed water on his face and used his finger as a toothbrush. It wasn't particularly effective, but at least his mouth would be more minty than not. He didn't want to overstep and take a shower, but he realized there was come drying on his crotch, which was a little gross, but some of that was Graham's, which made it inherently hot. He was also kind of proud; he wouldn't be messy if he hadn't had sex. Yeah, sure, they hadn't engaged in the most comprehensive sexual act, but to a twenty-four-year-old virgin, naked hand jobs counted for quite a lot.

He settled for using a washcloth to wipe himself down, rinsed it out, and left it drying on the shower bar. He put his boxers back on, waffled a bit, then put his T-shirt on as well.

He hoped his choice of pajamas worked and was reassured when he went back into the room and saw that Graham had put on a loose gray tank top. He was still wearing the briefs and the whole ensemble was ridiculously hot. He remembered what he'd thought that morning seeing Graham for the first time—that he could have been a model. Or a hooker. He exiled that last thought, though he wished J.R. well, wherever he was. But the other part was true. Jake was instantly jealous of anyone who'd ever gotten to see Graham like this, half-dressed and post-orgasm.

Graham smiled at Jake, took a small bag into the bathroom with him. Jake heard water running while he tidied his shoes and jeans and pulled back the covers on the bed. He froze before he got in—would Graham have a side preference? He was still looking down at the mattress indecisively when Graham came out of the bathroom wearing slim, rectangular glasses.

"Are you trying to kill me?" Jake asked, before he remembered. "Wait, I forgot you wear contacts."

Graham put the bag down on the nightstand, touched the front of his glasses, adorkably pushing them up his nose a fraction. "I do."

Jake felt hot all over. "Well, I like the glasses."

Graham's gaze dropped to the vicinity of Jake's waistband. Maybe slightly lower. His smile was faint. "Um. That's good." His voice was really low and Jake realized a couple of things at once. He was getting hard again, and Graham could tell. Maybe he liked it.

"Uh, which side of the bed do you want?" Was it weird to pretend he wasn't getting an erection? Were they supposed to acknowledge it?

"I don't care," Graham said with a hint of amusement. "Whatever makes you comfortable."

Jake faltered. He wasn't comfortable. He was turned

on and decidedly out of his comfort zone and his heart was so full of feelings for the man on the other side of the bed that he didn't know what to do with. He felt so...*good*. It was disorienting. And he was about to go to sleep in a different bed than he'd woken up in, which was new.

"I'll just...." He clumsily got on the bed, pulled the covers up to his waist, arousal taking a back seat to awkwardness.

Graham took off his glasses and set them on the nightstand, then followed him into bed and turned off the light. A slight reddish glow emanated from the smoke detector and the parking lot lights seeped in under the door, but the room was otherwise dark. Jake blinked, lay his head on the pillow, and turned toward Graham. He could make out his profile in the dark, the edge of his bare shoulder. He heard the rustle of sheets as Graham settled. Graham's foot brushed against Jake's shin, and he yanked his leg away instinctively, feeling immediately childish.

"Sorry, I—"

"Hey, it's okay." Then Graham was stroking his arm, as if calming a spooked horse. "Let's get some sleep."

"Right." Jake was both so exhausted and so wired he didn't think he'd be sleeping for a while.

"Unless—"

"Unless?"

"Can I kiss you goodnight?" Graham asked.

Jake let out an unidentifiable sound—half sob, half moan. He tipped his head forward, surprised when he encountered Graham's chest. They were closer together than he'd realized.

"What is it is?" Graham was all concern and the hand that had been on his arm came around to rub circles on his back.

"Nothing," Jake mumbled into Graham's chest, unable to explain that this was all too wonderful and that he was experiencing happiness overload, because that was just too embarrassing.

"Hey, you can talk to me. If we're...together...I want to know, you know?"

Jake breathed in the clean laundry scent of Graham's shirt, then shifted an inch to the side and breathed in the muskier scent of his armpit, overlaid with the remnants of his spicy deodorant. "You smell good." His voice was muffled, but Graham seemed to hear him.

He chuckled lightly. "Thanks. You smell good, too."

How was he so perfect? Jake pulled back from the warm embrace of Graham's body because this was important. "Graham?"

"Yes?"

"I'm happy." The words came out broken and miserable.

Graham didn't respond right away, and Jake felt like a spoiled brat for being difficult instead of going to sleep like a regular person. His eyes had adjusted to the dim light, and he could see Graham more clearly now. He was biting his lip.

"It's okay, babe," Graham said finally. "It's okay to be happy."

"It's just a lot," Jake whispered.

"I know."

Jake worried Graham was going to come to his senses

and realize Jake wasn't worth all this effort, but then he kept talking. "I remember when Mitch and I were first getting together how intense it all was. I was younger than you, and so nervous, so worried about fucking it up. But look, you don't have to worry about that. We're just going to take things one step at a time. Slow, remember?"

He sounded collected and sure and Jake appreciated his trying to make him feel better, but— "Slow is hard when I feel like this," he said.

"Like what?"

"Like..." He couldn't tell Graham he loved him. Not yet. Not within twenty-four hours of laying eyes on him for the first time, no matter how long they'd known each other. "Like, yeah, it's intense, and who knows how much time we're going to be able to spend together. You're going home tomorrow, right?"

"Yeah, I have to work. But we'll figure it out. I can come next weekend, maybe."

Jake ignored the stab of disappointment that he'd have to say goodbye to Graham in a matter of hours. "This is what I mean. You're probably right, slow makes sense, but I don't feel sensible right now." He gathered all his confusion and longing and love and kissed Graham, open-mouthed and eager. Graham responded instantly, kissing him back. Then they were scrabbling at each other, hands everywhere and Jake's erection was back with a vengeance.

He was happy, but the purity of being with someone he knew he loved was tinged with desperation and a little recklessness. They hadn't figured everything out and a part of Jake didn't believe this wouldn't all evaporate in the morning. His hand found Graham's cock through his underwear; it plumped under his hand.

There was no non-dorky way he could think of to ask, so he just went for it. He whispered into Graham's ear. "Can I give you a blow job?"

Graham shuddered and shifted closer. "Only if you want to, okay?"

In response, Jake slid down the bed. Graham pushed his briefs down his thighs. It was dark enough that Jake wasn't hung up on what it all looked like. He'd never done this before, and he was self-conscious as it was without worrying about Graham's view.

He couldn't see very well, but he could smell Graham, an earthy scent he found improbably appealing. He touched him with his hand first. The soft, trimmed thatch of hair at the base of his cock was a little damp. He must have wiped himself down, too, after their earlier encounter. He guided the tip of Graham's cock to his mouth, pausing for a moment to gather himself before he stuck his tongue out and licked the head, as if it was an ice cream cone. It tasted salty and clean and better than any ice cream Jake had ever had.

"Mmm." He went back for another taste. If he'd had any doubt about how much he would enjoy this, it was obliterated in the long minutes he spent licking and sucking on the head of Graham's beautiful cock, his hand loosely wrapped around the base as he worked his way up to taking more of his—boyfriend's?—erection into his mouth. He'd gotten around halfway down the shaft when he had the hang of it well enough to pay attention to other things besides the sensation of sucking cock, namely, Graham's stream of words that hadn't let up since the moment he'd started, only now Jake had the bandwidth to hear what he was saying.

"...perfect, fuck, your mouth, it's so hot. I knew your mouth would be sweet when I first saw you, but I didn't know how fucking talented it would be. Just like that, gorgeous. Don't stop, please, never stop. Damn, that's good..."

Jake pulled off long enough to say, "Fuck, Graham, I would have suggested this a lot sooner if I knew it would get you to talk that much."

"Shut up," Graham muttered, but there was a smile in his voice.

Jake obeyed him by putting his mouth back to the job at hand. Graham was still talking, his hips bucking minutely up, as if he was holding himself back from thrusting harder, which Jake appreciated. Maybe one day he'd be able to take everything Graham could give him, but this was already overwhelming in the best possible way.

"Babe, gorgeous, can I—" Graham's hands came up and rested lightly on Jake's head. One hand tentatively carded through his hair. It felt fucking fantastic. Jake leaned into Graham's touch and made a sound of assent. Graham tightened his hold a bit, which felt even better. Huh. Jake apparently liked having his hair touched, if not outright pulled.

"You like that?" Graham asked, husky and needy at the same time.

Jake pulled off again. His jaw was getting tired, but he didn't want to stop. Still, he hadn't anticipated the difficulty in communicating while giving head. "I like it. I want you to keep doing that and then come in my mouth." He surprised himself with his directness, but, what the hell. He *did* want Graham to keep touching him and come in his mouth.

"Jesus, fuck." Graham did as instructed, the pads of his fingers rubbing against Jake's scalp, strands of Jake's hair in between. Jake started sucking again, hollowing out his cheeks as best he could around Graham's girth. Graham babbled away as he pistoned shallowly into Jake's mouth. "I'm going to come, sweetheart. Are you sure you want—"

Jake sucked harder. Graham's hold tightened just as his words turned into moans and Jake tasted the first splash of come as it burst out of Graham and onto his tongue. Liquid flooded his mouth. It was bitter and salty and warm. He swallowed it instinctively, most of it anyway. Graham pulled out as the last pulses hit Jake's lips, coating them and hitting his chin.

He wiped his mouth with the back of his hand, swallowing again as he considered the aftertaste. Not exactly cheesecake, but not terrible. A little thrill went up his spine knowing he had a bit of Graham inside his body.

"Fuck." Graham flopped backward, his head hitting the pillow, an arm over his eyes.

Jake laughed and ignored the painful hardness of his own cock as he tucked Graham's back inside his briefs.

"You actually sucked my brains out of my dick."

"You're welcome?" Jake said, lifting in the end into a question.

"Definitely," Graham said. "And I'm gonna get you back in two seconds, I swear."

Jake belatedly remembered that Graham had been up since early and driven a couple hundred miles to see him, then had two orgasms. He laid down, kissed Graham's shoulder. "It's okay. I'm good."

"No, I'm good for it," Graham said. Then he yawned.

"You know it's not a quid pro quo thing, right?" Jake said.

"I know. I want to get my mouth on you so bad, you don't even know. But it's not fair how good you were at that. It's all I'm going to be thinking about, every minute of every day."

Jake's ebullience at succeeding at his first blow job faded at the reminder they were going separate ways in the morning. "It's okay. Something to look forward to," he said, trying to be mature about this.

"No, come here," Graham said, tugging at Jake's shirt. "Give me a chance."

Jake laughed. "You sure? We could just go to sleep."

"Come on. Feed me your cock."

The dirty request made Jake's blood run hot. "Yeah?"

"Yeah. Put it in my mouth."

Jake shuffled up the bed as Graham scooted down. They met in the middle, Graham on his back looking up at Jake. He opened his mouth, stuck his tongue out, and licked his lips. Jake was a goner. He leaned forward, whipping his cock out of his boxers, until the tip of it connected with Graham's bottom lip. Graham nodded, and Jake went a little further. The next second, Graham sucked the length of him almost to the back of his throat with one smooth motion and Jake shouted in pleasure.

"Holy hell, Graham, that feels incredible," he said. Graham kept at it, his cheekbones and the pout of his perfect lips the only thing Jake could really see in the dark. Jake was perpendicular to Graham's face, but it didn't seem to matter. Graham's technique was flawless as he sucked and reached out with one hand to spur Jake on by grabbing his hip and squeezing. It didn't take long before the wet heat and the fact that it was Graham, beautiful, funny, sweet, kind Graham who was sucking Jake like he was the best thing he'd ever tasted, had him shouting again, coming in long waves of pleasure. Graham kept his mouth firmly attached until it was all over, then he let Jake go with a wet pop and smack of his lips.

"Okay, we're even. My brains are fucking goo," Jake said, collapsing next to Graham halfway down the bed.

"I thought you said it wasn't quid pro quo." Graham's voice was shredded. Jake hadn't thought it was possible for him to sound sexier, but he was wrong.

He giggled. "I have no comeback. Brains goo. Now sleep." He halfheartedly pulled up the waistband of his boxers and patted Graham's arm.

"Yeah, sleep."

They found a pillow each and the last thing Jake was aware of before he fell asleep was Graham rolling over to place a kiss on his cheek.

SIXTEEN

JAKE HADN'T EXPECTED to sleep well, considering he was in a strange bed in a strange place with another more-than-six-foot-tall man, but apparently two back-to-back orgasms were better exercise than the animal shelter because he passed out and didn't wake up again until he heard Graham open the door to the bathroom. He cracked his eyes open. The room was semi-dark, bright white light edging around the curtained front windows.

"Morning, sunshine," Graham said. He was almost too good looking in the same dark jeans from last night and a different button-down shirt, light green this time, sleeves rolled up to the elbows. He sat on a chair and tied the laces on his shoes.

"Morning." Jake rubbed the sleep out of his eyes. "You're still here."

Graham cocked his head. "Why wouldn't I be?"

"I thought maybe I dreamed you," he said before he could stop himself.

Graham just smiled. "If you did, then we're having the same dream. A fucking great dream."

Jake marveled at Graham's words. God, he loved him.

He sat up and wished he had clean clothes. His tight jeans would have to do. He wriggled into them while Graham gathered his things and stowed them in his overnight bag.

"When do you have to leave?"

"I should get on the road after breakfast."

"Okay. What do you feel like eating?"

"Whatever you want."

"The Apple Pan has the best eggs in town."

"The cute place we ate lunch at yesterday? Sounds perfect."

Jake used the bathroom quickly, finger combing his hair, wishing he had a razor. He could ask to use Graham's but even though they'd had their cocks down each other's throats last night, he didn't know if they were at that level of intimacy yet. Instead, he cleaned up as best he could, went out to put his shoes and jacket back on.

"Meet you there?" he asked, as Graham looked up from checking his phone.

"Yes, but first I need to do something very important." Graham crossed the room in two big strides. He tilted his head up and kissed Jake sweetly, once, twice, three times, until Jake was ready to melt into a puddle of want.

"There," Graham said, stepping back. "Now we can go."

"You sure?" Jake asked, not even caring how breathy

his voice sounded. "I mean, I'm pretty sure they won't kick us out until eleven."

Graham laughed. "If we go back to bed, I'm never going to want to leave. Please, help me out here, sugar."

Jake only agreed because Graham was right. If they went back to bed now, it would take an act of God to pry him out of Graham's arms.

THE APPLE PAN was busy with the Sunday brunch crowd. Liana bustled around refilling coffee mugs, but when she spotted them she motioned to the last empty two-top, smack in the center of the room. Graham took the chair facing the door, and Jake slid into the one opposite, his back to the entrance. It made him feel conspicuous to be in the middle of the diner wearing yesterday's clothes, with the hottest guy in Apple Vale as his breakfast date.

"Is everyone staring at us, or am I being paranoid?" he whispered to Graham as they looked at their menus.

Liana fluttered by, dropping coffee in their cups. "Be back to take your order in a sec, boys."

Graham glanced around casually. "I think everyone is focused on getting their caffeine fix, but if they're looking at us, it's because you're glowing."

Jake hadn't been blushing before, but at Graham's comment his cheeks burned. "What?"

"It's adorable. And I know I'm being a sap, but I have to get my fill. I'll be thinking about your dimples all the way home, sweetheart."

Jake was torn between wanting to hide his head in his hands and preen under Graham's praise. He felt the minutes they had left slipping between his fingers, so he decided to pretend they were the only two people in the diner. "You keep calling me things."

Graham raised his eyebrows.

"You know, endearments. Sweetheart and stuff," Jake said, voice barely above a whisper.

"I'm trying them all out until I find the one that fits best." Graham winked. "Cream for your coffee, honey?"

Jake wrinkled his nose. "My mom calls me Honey Cakes sometimes, so maybe not honey."

Graham laughed. "Noted. I suppose it's only fair you get a say in your own pet name. Also, that's extremely cute."

Jake took a sip of his coffee. He was relaxing and about to tell Graham about his favorite Apple Pan omelet when he heard a voice behind him.

"Honey Cakes!"

Jake whipped his head around. It took him a second to understand what he was seeing. Liv stood behind him, her eyes wide. What was she doing here?

"Mom?"

"Jake, hi!" His mom's voice was unnaturally pitched, but that wasn't the only thing about her that was a little off. Her normally tidy hair was sticking up in spikes all over her head, and—was she wearing the same clothes she'd left for work in yesterday?

"Hi." He saw her glance behind him to his table companion. "Um. Mom. This is Graham."

"Your computer friend?" Liv asked.

Nothing like your mom to make you feel twelve years old. "Yes, Mom, my computer friend. He came for a visit."

"How nice!" she said, sounding more like herself. "Pleased to meet you, Graham."

Jake turned and threw Graham an apologetic look, but he was already standing up, smiling politely, and offering Liv his hand to shake. "Pleasure to meet you, Mrs. Crane."

"Liv, please."

There was an awkward moment of silence during which Jake finally realized there was a man standing a foot behind his mother who was watching them as if he had a vested interest in the proceedings. He didn't recognize the man—he definitely wasn't a coworker of his mom's at the nonprofit she worked at. He looked too young to be a friend. Standing there in a muscle tee and jeans, the man was about Graham's height, his hair a shade or two lighter that Graham's, his face a little more rugged, but they could have been cousins. In fact, if Jake wasn't already head over heels for Graham, he definitely would have looked at the man twice.

What on earth was this guy doing with his mother?

Liana broke the impasse when she hurried over. "Hey, Mrs. Crane. We're kinda slammed. Do you want to drag chairs over and join these boys?"

Liv looked uncertainly over her shoulder at the man.

"That'll be fine," the stranger said.

"Mom?" Jake was beyond confused. He stood up, as if that would help matters.

Graham, meanwhile, simply got up and grabbed two chairs from a stack behind the door. He shifted Jake's chair around the table so they were sharing a corner and set the others across.

Liv glanced at the guy, who smiled broadly and sat down in the chair next to Graham. She shrugged and took the remaining chair. Jake sank into his, glad that he was at least closer to Graham now, who patted his knee under the table.

"I'm Graham," he said, offering his hand to the stranger.

"Jeremy Robinson, Junior," the guy said.

Jake narrowed his eyes at Jeremy Robinson, Junior, as he connected the dots. "Let me guess, you go by J.R.?"

"Got it in one," J.R. said. "But my friends call me Jeremy."

"Friends? Like my mom?" Jake bit out.

"So, it's a kind of funny story," Liv said, her cheeks coloring.

Jake wanted to be angry. Or amused. Or concerned. But he was too dazed for any other emotion besides bewilderment. "Go on," Jake said. "I'm all ears."

"Well. I got off work early yesterday and went home to see if you wanted to get a birthday lunch. You said you didn't have any plans so I..." Liv trailed off and looked at Graham, her gaze turning speculative. "I suppose you went out. But there was Jeremy, waiting outside our house. He said he was waiting for the lady of the house and that someone named Chip had told him to meet her at this address."

"The lady of the house? But—" Damn Chip, that phrasing was probably some kind of joke on his part. He wondered if J.R. was even into guys. It would be like

Chip to accidentally hire a straight hooker to deflower his male friend. Though maybe it didn't matter to J.R.

"I told him there was some mistake, and we got to talking. And well, you weren't around, and I was hungry, so I asked Jeremy if he wanted to get some lunch. Which we did. And, um, we sort of. Hit it off." Liv looked down at the table.

"Your mother is a special person," J.R.—*Jeremy* said. He smiled at Liv with lots of teeth and Jake recoiled. He hadn't seen anyone look at his mother like that since his dad. Liv looked back at Jeremy with pink cheeks and a smile that made her look ten years younger.

"She certainly is," Jake said tightly. "Mom, could we talk outside?" What if this guy was scamming his mom or holding something over her? She needed to know what he did for a living. Sure, she didn't seem any worse for wear except for being slightly flustered, but that didn't mean anything.

Liv frowned. "Why?"

"Just. I need to talk to you."

"Can it wait, Honey Cakes? Oh, is this your coffee? Can I have a sip?" She took a big sip from his mug. "That's good."

"You guys have been hanging out since lunch yesterday?" Jake asked, even though he already sort of knew the answer.

"Well. Yes. I thought you would have noticed I didn't come home last night. We drove by the house at one point, and I saw the truck in the driveway, so I wasn't worried about you."

"Oh my God—you were at the Shadow Brook Motel

last night. I saw your Volvo there." Jake put a hand on his forehead, grabbed Graham's mug of coffee and took a big gulp. "We need more coffee."

"What were you doing at the motel?" Liv asked. She glanced at Graham. "Where are you visiting from again, Graham?"

"Boston."

"That's a long drive." Liv said.

"Slow down, babe," Graham said, as Jake took another big sip from his mug. "Not on an empty stomach."

"Where's Liana? We should order," Jake said, looking around the diner. He felt a little wild. There was too much to process.

"So all four of us put up at the motel last night?" Jeremy said, grinning wide. "Comfy beds, right?" he said to nobody in particular.

Jake closed his eyes. This was just too weird. He shoved back from the table. Graham was looking at him with concern, but Liv and Jeremy only seemed to have eyes for each other, and it was disorienting.

"I'm just going to get some air," he said. "Order me an omelet, please?"

Graham nodded. "Sure thing."

Jake had no fear that whatever Graham ordered Jake would like. They seemed to enjoy the same foods if their restaurant orders over the past two days were any sign. He escaped out the diner's front door, past the line of people waiting their turn for a table. The day was already heating up. The forecast was for an even warmer day than yesterday. He fanned himself with his hand. Why was this bothering him so much? If his mom was happy, he should be happy for her.

"You okay, babe?"

He turned and Graham was just—there. Live, in the flesh, and already so important to Jake he was afraid losing him would be too painful to bear.

He didn't answer right away, just pulled Graham in for a hug. Graham came easily, hugging him back like they'd done it every day of their lives. He supposed they had done it both days since they'd met. But Graham was leaving soon, and who knew how many days would pass, hugless, before they met again?

"Hey, what's wrong?" Graham asked softly.

"I'm really going to miss you," Jake said, whispering it into Graham's hair. Graham tightened his hold in response.

"Me too."

They ended the hug. Jake was still aware of eyes on them, and he couldn't fall apart just yet. "But that's not all. My mom. Since my dad died, she's been on like two dates with drips her friends set her up with. And suddenly she's spending the night in a motel with *that* guy?"

"Yeah, the motel was an awkward coincidence, but he didn't seem so bad," Graham said.

"Graham, he's a hooker."

"I think the preferred term is sex worker," Graham said with a quirk of his lips.

"He's a sex worker, then," Jake said, "and I'm not joking."

Graham laughed. "What? How do you know?"

"Because Chip hired him to be my birthday present. When you showed up yesterday, I thought you were him. But you were you. And he met my mom and must have thought she was his client and now my mom is infatuated with a sex worker from Manhattan. How is this happening?"

Graham's smile faded as Jake's twisted tale went on. When Jake finally stopped talking, his smile had disappeared altogether.

"You thought I was someone else? For how long?"

"Um. I realized over lunch yesterday."

"Lunch?" Graham's eyes went wide. "Seriously? Were you ever going to say anything?"

Jake was out of his depth. Was Graham mad? What did you do when your boyfriend was pissed at you? "I don't know. Once I figured out who you were, it didn't seem important."

"Not important that the first two hours we spent together you thought I was a completely different person? A hooker?"

"I thought the preferred term was sex worker," Jake tried.

Graham glared at him. "It feels like you lied to me, Jake. And I get that this is new for you, and hard, but I need to be able to trust you."

"I'm so sorry, Graham," Jake said. "I'd never found myself in that situation before, obviously."

Graham bit his lip. It was still sexy, but also rather sad. The coffee in Jake's otherwise empty stomach sloshed around uncomfortably.

"Why the hell would Chip send you a sex worker for your birthday present?"

"Why does Chip do anything? He thought he was being helpful and going about it in the most unhelpful way possible."

Graham sighed. "He's the one who gave me your address, by the way. It didn't occur to me to check with him about conflicts with sex workers in your schedule."

Jake wasn't sure if this was Graham forgiving him, but at least they were talking through it.

"You can see why I was acting so weird at first."

"I thought you were charming," Graham said.

"Oh my God, this is why I love you. You always say the right thing. Eventually."

"What. You love me?"

Jake froze. He hadn't exactly meant for it to slip out like that. "Is that okay?"

Graham's expression softened. "It's okay," he said, smile growing. "In fact, it's really convenient. Because I love you, too."

Jake laughed and couldn't resist yanking his boyfriend back into his arms. He even kissed him on the mouth. Whoever saw them and didn't approve could go to hell. His boyfriend loved him. That was a kiss-worthy occasion if there ever was one.

Graham kissed him back. "I love you, Jake."

"I love you, Graham." His heart felt light and heavy at once. "I wish you didn't have to go."

"I know, babe. But we'll work it out."

Jake was about to suggest they look at their calendars

together when his stomach rumbled loudly. "Sorry. I guess I need that omelet."

They walked shoulder to shoulder back inside, only to be confronted with Liv and Jeremy sucking face in the middle of the Apple Pan. Jake and Graham exchanged a glance.

"Maybe we should go someplace else?" Graham suggested.

"Definitely."

SEVENTEEN

SAYING goodbye to Graham was harder than it should have been considering Jake had only really met him twenty-four hours ago. Then again, a lot had happened in those twenty-four hours. Mistaken identities, confusing first impressions, dog slobber, meddling grandmothers, soul-baring speeches, and falling in love. Not to mention the amazing kisses and the incredible sex. Yeah, Jake's twenty-fourth birthday was one for the books.

But his birthday was over.

They found a less-than-awesome meal at the donut shop on the other end of Main Street—lukewarm breakfast burritos and weak coffee. They ate knee to knee at a tiny table on the sidewalk outside. Graham had relaxed since Jake's confession. He agreed that the outlandish plot twist of hiring someone to have sex with Jake as a birthday present sounded like something Chip would have a hand in.

"Remember when he tried to get us to invest in that sketchy traveling dance troupe?" Graham asked.

"Oh yeah. The ones who were doing an off-brand version of *Hamilton?* Looking back, they were probably strippers."

"You didn't give him any money, did you?"

Jake snorted. "Hell, no. Why, did you?"

"Please. Though Chip is a decent friend. He gave me your address."

"You could have just asked me. And, like, told me you were coming. Then we could have avoided some of the nonsense." Jake couldn't really complain about the way things had turned out, even if his mom having a one-night stand with Jeremy was still wigging him out.

"I know. I was scared. But I had good reason. This—" Graham gestured between them "—it's the real thing, babe. It's only right that we be scared. That we take it seriously."

Jake's stomach flipped. Graham looked so solemn. So grown up. It was a strange sensation, to be someone who someone like Graham wanted. "I know. I do."

Graham nodded, as if something had been decided. "Okay. We'll figure it out. I'll call you when I get home, okay?"

"Okay."

"And you can call me, or text me, whenever you want."

"Yeah?" Jake liked the idea of being able to talk to Graham on the phone instead of only messaging with him.

"In fact, I'll be missing you so bad, you probably won't have a chance to call, because I'll already have called you."

"So, you're saying you're going to be clingy?" Jake teased.

"Clingy and long distance—wow, what a sexy combination," Graham joked.

"It's okay. I have a feeling I'll be happy to take you any way I can get you."

"Well, I'm really looking forward to you taking me." Graham waggled his eyebrows.

Jake laughed, even as his cheeks warmed at the implications. "Me too."

"Are you sure you're going to be okay?"

"I'll be okay," Jake said. "I promise."

They hugged by Graham's car. Jake tried to memorize his smell, the pressure of his arms around his body. He kissed the side of Graham's head, brushing his nose briefly through the short hairs there.

"Drive safe," he said, pulling back far enough to look Graham in the eye.

"I will." Graham's mouth turned down at the corners.

Jake wanted so much to kiss him until he was smiling again, but they were in the parking lot of a strip mall, and he wasn't quite ready for that kind of public statement. Still, there was no one within earshot. "I love you."

The smile came back. "Love you." Graham got in the Civic and started it quickly, as if he could force himself to leave if he just did it fast enough. Jake caught him swiping a thumb under his eye.

He waved. Graham's smile wobbled, and then he pulled out of the parking spot. Jake watched until the car was gone.

His heart felt funny, the happiness of having Graham

as more than a chatting partner on a screen warring with the pain of watching him drive away. He reminded himself that he wasn't driving out of his life, just to Boston. Jake had to believe he would see him again.

Even if part of him worried he wouldn't be so lucky.

THE HOUSE WAS empty when he got back; his mom had clearly not returned. Was she still with Jeremy? He decided he couldn't worry about his mom's love life when all he wanted to do was curl into a ball and hide in the dark until Graham came back.

But he was trying to do things differently now. Instead of crawling into bed, he took a shower, even though scrubbing Graham's scent off his skin made Jake long for him all over again.

He hunched over to see himself in the mirror as he combed his hair, shaved. God, he was sick of this tiny bathroom, of his childish bedroom. He turned on his computer, ignored his messages, and started streaming Creedence. The opening licks of "Lookin' Out My Back-door" made him smile. They had been his dad's favorite band. He still had his dad's CCR tapes in the truck. He remembered whenever his dad popped one in, he'd say, "I hate the fuckin' Eagles, man." Jake would laugh every time at the non sequitur. It had shocked him when he got older to realize his dad had been quoting *The Big Lebowski* all that time.

He surveyed the room, the posters on the wall, the bookshelves filled with graphic novels, comics, books, and video games. He opened his closet and took in the exten-sive collection of flannels.

Not only was he a year older, but he was also going to start a new job soon. He'd have his master's degree in a matter of weeks. He had a *boyfriend*.

There was no time like the present. He ran to the basement for some empty cardboard boxes, bounded back up, and started filling them.

Jake Crane was leveling up.

WHEN HIS PHONE RANG, Jake was shocked to find hours had passed. He barely registered Graham's name on the screen before answering breathlessly, "Hello?"

"Hey, babe, I'm home." Graham's voice, already so dear to him, came over the phone smooth and deep.

"This is the first time I'm hearing your voice on the phone."

"Yeah. You sound good, Jake."

"Thanks. You, too."

They were both quiet for a few seconds. It seemed Graham's occasional shyness wasn't magically canceled during phone calls.

Jake cleared a space on his bed. "How was your drive?"

"Boring. Fine. I thought about you a lot."

"Yeah?"

"A lot about last night." Graham's voice dropped and sent a shiver through Jake.

"Oh. That was pretty great." He rolled his eyes at his understatement.

"Yeah. So. What have you been up to, gorgeous?"

Jake swore he was blushing even though there was no one around to overhear Graham's endearment. "Actually, I've been packing."

"No shit? How's that going?"

"It's good. I've lived in this room my entire life. It's overdue for an overhaul, anyway."

"I wish I'd seen your room before you dismantled it."

Jake looked around. It was still his room, just pared down. It looked more adult. "No, I'm glad you didn't. I've been stuck in the past for too long. And you're part of my future."

"I better be."

Jake smiled. "I miss you."

Graham let out a big breath. "Fuck. Me too. This already sucks."

"You said we'd figure it out and we will," Jake said with more confidence than he felt.

"Yeah. We will."

Jake heard the rattle of the front door through his open bedroom door. "I think my mom's finally home."

"Oh. I'll let you go. Text me later?"

"Sure." He hesitated. They'd said I love you a few times, but he wasn't sure if they were the type of couple who said it every time they got off the phone or what. His parents had certainly said it to each other so much it felt like second nature to sign off with it now, but he didn't want to—

"Love you, babe," Graham said. "Have a good night."

"Love you, too. Good night, Graham."

He ended the call smiling from ear to ear. He tromped down the stairs. "Mom?"

Liv was putting her purse down on the table by the stairs. She looked up and gave him a tentative smile. "Hi."

"Um. Can we talk?"

She looked at him steadily for a moment. "Sure. Of course. Let me get a cup of tea?"

He followed her into the kitchen, sat on a white wooden stool at the island. She moved around the kitchen efficiently, filling up the electric kettle, selecting a mug from the cupboard. He'd seen her make herself a cup of tea a million times in his life. Tonight, he really looked at her. She was his mom, and he loved her, but maybe he'd never really seen her as her own person. She'd always been his mom, his dad's wife, then his widow. Nana's daughter-in-law who Nana loved as well as her own children. She'd been young when she'd had him. She wasn't even fifty yet. It wasn't fair that his dad had died so young, but Jake realized his mom needed to move on just as much as he did.

"I love you, Mom." He said it all the time, but it felt different when it wasn't an automatic reflex.

Liv was unwrapping a tea bag, paused to look at him, so much love in her eyes. "I love you, too, Honey Cakes."

"Water's ready." He nodded at the kettle.

She filled her mug, then took the stool on the other side of the island so they were facing each other. "I guess I know what you want to talk about."

"Really?" Jake figured she would have drawn some conclusions about Graham's presence at breakfast, but he was pretty sure what he had to say was going to come as a revelation.

"You've got every right to be upset about seeing me and Jeremy together. I'm sorry about springing it on you like that, but it all happened so fast. I hope you understand I wasn't trying to hurt you."

"What?" Jake shook his head. "No, I wasn't—well, I was surprised. But I was going to talk to you about Graham. And me."

"Oh? What's that?"

Jake's gut swooped with unexpected nerves. "We're together now. He's my boyfriend."

His mom had known he was gay since before he did, but he'd never had the occasion to utter those words before. Her reaction didn't disappoint. She grinned and her eyes welled up with tears. She was laughing and crying at the same time.

"That's so great. I'm so happy for you. Oh my, he's very handsome, isn't he? How did it happen? When? Is he still in Apple Vale? Can I meet him properly?"

Jake laughed and put up a hand to stop her questions. "Mom, calm down. One thing at a time, okay?"

"You're right. Sorry. This is just really fantastic." She grinned.

Jake knew part of her happiness was that he'd been alone for so long. He knew she worried about him and his social skills.

"The short version is we've liked each other for a while, but he finally decided to come meet me in person. He drove here yesterday and surprised me. We ended up spending the day together. He even met Nana." He smiled, thinking about Nana's future reaction to this development. "Anyway, we're going to have to be long distance for a while, but we really care about each other."

"He seemed nice in the two minutes I spent with him today."

"He's really nice. He's a teacher, I think I've mentioned that before. And he's really sweet and he —" Jake swallowed against a lump in his throat "—he really likes me, Mom."

"Of course he does," Liv said softly. "You deserve the best guy in the world. I hope he can live up to my expectations for your partner."

"Graham is—he's kind of perfect, without being actually perfect," he added, thinking about the emotional fits and starts of the past day and a half. "But we're really invested in making this work."

"Boston's so far away," she said, frowning a little. "But I'm sure if you are committed and communicate, you guys can make long distance work."

"Thanks." He drummed his fingers on the island, working up to the next part. "And, well, this is something I've been needing to do, and Graham coming into my life just gave me a push. I need to move out."

The tears were back, but Liv nodded bravely. "I know you do, Honey Cakes."

Jake got up and went around the island to put his arm around his diminutive mother.

She sagged into his side. "I'm so happy for you."

"Yeah, I can tell from all the tears," he said lightly.

"No, really." She sniffed. "You're growing up, Jake, and I'm so proud."

"'Thanks, Mom."

They held each other for another minute before Liv brushed the tears off her face and turned toward the fridge. "Can I make you some dinner?" she said briskly, in a tone that told him she was trying to hold things together until she was alone later and able to truly fall apart over her only child leaving home.

"Sure, if you're making some for yourself."

"I'm starving. I missed lunch."

"What have you been doing all day?" Jake asked, before he remembered the last time he'd seen her was attached at the lips to a guy she'd only met the day before. "Never mind—don't answer that."

Liv took him at his word and pulled the cake box out of the fridge. "What's this?"

"Oh. Graham bought me a birthday cheesecake."

She lifted her eyebrows. "Cheesecake, seriously? Oh, Jake, you better marry this guy."

He scoffed, but if was being perfectly honest, he agreed with his mom on that point.

"Call me crazy, but cheesecake kind of sounds good for dinner," she said.

"If that's crazy, I don't want to be sane," Jake said definitively.

They sat in the kitchen together, eating cheesecake straight out of the box.

THEY'D WORKED their way through too much of the cheesecake when Liv's cell phone buzzed on the kitchen counter. She grabbed it and read the screen. The smile that came onto her face was sly and private, and Jake thought he recognized the look. His mother was smitten. The cake turned to lead in his stomach.

"Is that Jeremy?" he asked cautiously.

"Um. Yeah." She put the phone down. "He's back in New York. But we're talking about meeting up soon. I thought I'd take the train down. It's been ages since I went to the city."

Jake was stunned. "Wait, you're planning to see him again?"

"I know it feels sudden, but I really like him." Liv seemed bashful, but also happy. "Since your dad I never felt a spark with anyone else. Being on my own these last few years has been nice in some ways. But Jeremy...he just lights me up."

"But he's—" Could he form the words he needed to

say before he died of embarrassment? He and his mom had always been able to talk about anything, but neither of them had sex lives to speak of before so something like this had never come up.

He bunted. "He's like twenty years younger than you!"

She rolled her eyes. "He's thirty-four, which makes him fourteen years younger, and yeah, that's a big gap, but it doesn't bother either of us. So, it shouldn't bother you."

"Okay. Fine." Jake mustered all his courage. "He's a prostitute, Mom."

She stopped in the act of putting their cheesecake forks in the dishwasher. "How did you know that?"

Wait—she knew? "It's a long story, but—"

"Oh my God—*that's* why he was at our house? He was there for you? Did you hire him? I thought he got his addresses mixed up or something and some bored house-wife was getting stood up."

"No! God. Mom. No." Jake sighed. How was this a conversation he was actually having with his mother? "You know my friend Chip?"

"Vaguely. The one who lives in Florida?"

"Yeah. They do things differently there, apparently. He hired J.R.—Jeremy—to come to our house as a birthday present for me. I had no idea, obviously. And when Graham showed up that morning, I thought he was—"

Liv's fingers flew to her mouth and she made a horri-fied noise. "Oh, no."

"Oh yes. I thought he was—but only for a little while

until I figured it out—and he knows everything now and it's all good, but I kind of forgot there was an actual sex worker who was supposed to be there until you showed up with him at the diner."

Liv slowly lowered her fingers. Then she laughed. "What the fuck?"

Jake let out a nervous laugh. His mom didn't swear around him much. "I know, right?"

When Liv had calmed down, she shook her head. "Well, I don't know what your friend Chip was thinking, but I'm glad you weren't here when Jeremy showed up."

"Me, too," Jake agreed fervently. He didn't want to imagine if he'd been off with Jeremy while Graham was knocking on his front door. The idea of missing out on Graham made him feel sick to his stomach, though that could have been too much cheesecake.

"To set your mind at ease, I know Jeremy is a sex worker. It's just a job. He's also a writer. He's got three science fiction books published, and he's working on the next one in the series. And I like him and I'm going to see him again and no exchange of money will take place, so you can take that look off your face right now, Jake Crane."

Jake schooled himself and tried to keep an open mind. "You guys must have done a lot of... talking."

"For your information, we did. I don't know how long this is going to last, and I really don't care. But I suppose I'm happy your friend Chip has weird boundaries because I needed a jolt and Jeremy jolted me. He jolted me good."

"Mom. Stop. I get it." Jake wanted to cry and laugh at

the same time. He settled on giving his mom another hug. "Then I'm happy for you. And I don't mind about any of it, really. As long as he treats you right, okay?"

"Good." Liv squeezed him back. "And thanks."

A WEEK PASSED FASTER than Jake anticipated. Maybe actively missing someone filled up the time quickly. Or maybe his life was simply time-consuming. He had school, his Grief Sucks shifts, searching for an apartment he could afford, his counseling sessions at the nursing home, his last few volunteer shifts at the animal shelter, plus some onboarding things for his upcoming job at the hospital. As he filled out paperwork, he wondered if he was making a mistake by taking this job. A part of him wanted to look for work in the Boston area instead.

He and Graham talked every day, which helped, sort of. Graham's voice was a velvet soft tease, and he didn't censor himself, telling Jake how much he missed him and hinting at the things they would do with each other when they were back in the same place. The calls always left Jake missing him worse than before.

Neither of them could get away for the upcoming weekend; he was disappointed to realize he'd have to wait at least another week to get his hands on his handsome boyfriend.

In the meantime, he sorted things out with Chip. Or tried to.

Chip: So how does it feel to have finally lost the V-Card, J-man?

Jake: Can you do humanity a favor and stop interfering in other people's sex lives, please?

Chip: Why? Was J.R. not good? He came recommended!!!

Jake: I'm going to tell you what happened so you can learn the error of your ways.

Jake: After you told me J.R. was coming a man showed up on my doorstep. I thought he was J.R.

Jake: But he was Graham.

Chip: Graham's a hooker?

Jake: The preferred term is sex worker. And no!!! He's not!!! He just happened to show up at the same time you sent me the weirdest birthday present ever. He even said you gave him my address.

Chip: Oh yeah!! Thought he wanted to send you a birthday card or something.

Jake: That would be a normal way for a friend to cele-brate another friend's birthday. Take notes.

Jake: Anyway, I thought Graham was J.R. at first, but eventually I figured it out. The good news is, Graham and I are together now.

Chip: Together?

Jake: Dating. Boyfriends.

Chip: Wow!!! That's amazing!!! You guys flirt enough online, shoulda seen that coming.

Chip: That's so great!!

Jake: Thanks. :)

Chip: So I guess you lost your V-card anyway??!!

Jake: No comment

Chip: No comment means yes. Woo hoo! That's my boy!
Jake: You are weirdly obsessed with my sex life.

There was a long pause before the next message came through.

Chip: Jake, you helped me through a tough time in my life and I'll always be grateful for that. I just want you to be happy, man.

Jake stared at the deeply sincere words on the screen. Chip had found the grief forum after his younger brother died in a boating accident that had left Chip injured, but alive. Sometimes Jake forgot how they became friends in the first place, months of Chip being difficult and extra as he worked through his survivor's guilt until ultimately accepting that he couldn't have done anything to save his brother's life. He used humor to deflect, but moments like this reminded Jake there was a human with genuine feelings under all the exclamation marks.

Jake: Thanks, Chip. I am happy.
Chip: Then I'm happy, too, man. Even if I wasted six hundred $$$
Jake: Six hundred dollars? I'll pay you back.
Chip: Nah, you ended up having a great birthday, it sounds like. Worth it. What happened to J.R., anyway?
Jake: So this is the weird part.
Jake: Don't judge.
Chip: Would I do that???

Jake: Actually, probably not. When J.R. showed up my mom came home, and somehow they met and J.R. thought he was there for her (lady of the house, really?) and long story short they started hanging out and I don't want to think about the details but she's visiting him in New York this weekend.

Chip: ?????!!!!!!

Chip: Your mom boned the hooker I got for you and now they're dating????

Jake: I would have said it differently, but

Jake: Yes

Chip: Go your mom! Two for one! I am like a matchmaking god!

Jake: How does this comedy of errors in any way make you a matchmaking god?

Chip: It just does, okay? Two happy couples because of the old Chipster!

Jake: That's not the lesson you were supposed to learn here.

Chip: Who else can I help in the name of love? Raj?

Jake: He already has a girlfriend—please stop. I beg you.

Chip: You're right. With great power comes great responsibility. I can't use my powers lightly.

Jake: Let's go with that. Just stop giving people my address. I'm going to be moving soon, anyway.

Chip: J-man, moving out. That's awesome!!!

Jake smiled. He hated to give Chip any credit, but Graham was right. He was a menace, but he was a good friend.

"THANKS FOR THE RIDE, HONEY CAKES." Liv hoisted her overnight case out of the bed of the truck as Jake idled in the train station parking lot. "I'll text you when I know which train I'm getting back."

"Be safe," Jake said. "Have fun."

"I will, on both counts, I promise." Liv blew him a kiss. He watched until she'd made it safely onto the platform, then made a U-turn out of the lot.

His mom was on her way to meet up with Jeremy in the city. Graham had an exhibition track meet all day today, Saturday, and Jake had to work Sunday. They were having trouble lining up their schedules. Boston was a four-hour drive, but it might as well have been a four-day trip. Long distance was no joke.

Since the day stretched out in front of him with no plans, besides a paper for his psych class he was nearly done with, he decided to swing by The Vale and visit his favorite septuagenarian.

He found Nana working on a puzzle in the rec room.

"Hey, Nana."

"Jake, this is a lovely surprise. You want to help me with the sky?"

Jake looked down at the puzzle, which was complete except for an expanse of sky. He looked at the remaining pieces. They all appeared to be an identical shade of blue.

"Uh. Sure." He fiddled with a few pieces listlessly.

"Where's your young man today?"

Jake had already filled her in on the bare bones of his and Graham's date at the steakhouse and their subsequent decision to try long distance. He sighed. "He's at home. In Boston."

"Why don't you go visit him?" She fitted a piece into place, grabbed another, and snapped it in.

Jake blinked. "I can't. He's busy. I'm busy. I'm trying to be an adult about this, but it really sucks."

Nana chuckled. "I'm glad for all this newfound maturity, Jake, but I hate to be the one to break it to you—being an adult does suck a lot of the time."

Jake groaned. "I don't know what I expected. We knew each other for three years and I never felt like this being apart from him. Obviously, meeting him changed things, but maybe some part of me thought if we loved—if we *cared* about each other enough, the distance wouldn't matter." He and Graham still signed off every phone call with "I love you," but that wasn't for public consumption.

Thankfully, Nana didn't comment on the slip. "That's a natural assumption. After all, you're a romantic, Jake."

"I am?"

"Don't you think one reason you waited so long before you put yourself out there for a relationship was because you were waiting for the right person?"

Jake had never thought about it like that. He'd always just felt out of place and alone.

"I know Apple Vale isn't the epicenter of culture, gay or otherwise, but you could have dated if you had wanted to. You could have moved away, could have gone into the city."

"Like my mom?" Jake winced at the sour note in his voice. He didn't begrudge his mom her happiness, even if he was still wrapping his head around *who* she'd chosen to be happy with, at least for the time being. And it wasn't the side gig as a sex worker thing. He was trying not to let it be about the age thing. Jeremy was an entire decade older than him. It wasn't *that* weird.

He was just jealous, because she was going to see the guy she liked this weekend. And he wasn't.

"Your mom is a grown-up, remember?" Nana said lightly. "And so are you, so you keep telling me. Act like one. Go after what you want. Life is hard enough. Stop letting being responsible keep you from being happy."

Jake let Nana's words sink in as he stared down at the puzzle. He stared for so long that his vision blurred, and the colors of the puzzle started swirling and bleeding together. It didn't matter. All he could see was Graham's face, anyway. All he wanted was a future where he and Graham could be together, a team of two, supporting each other, loving each other. Building a life, getting a dog, maybe one day deciding to have a kid or two. He imagined Graham with a tow-headed baby in his arms and just about melted on the spot.

Nana was right. He'd waited long enough, and now that he had the one he'd been waiting for, he didn't want to wait any longer. He felt his truck keys in his pocket, glanced at the clock on the wall behind Nana. If he hurried, he might get there by the time the track meet ended. If Graham minded him just showing up, well, he couldn't really object, since he'd done it first, right?

He gave his grandmother a brief, tight hug. "Thanks, Nana. You gave me the push I needed—again. I love you."

"I love you, too. Say hi to Graham for me."

"I will."

NINETEEN

JAKE WAS GETTING gas at a travel stop on the turnpike when he realized that while he'd had the presence of mind to go home and grab some clothes and his toothbrush and he'd even texted Liv to let her know he wouldn't be able to pick her up at the train station the next day, after he'd called in fake sick to work and asked his teacher for an extension on his paper, he didn't actually know where he was going. He didn't have Graham's address.

He could call him, but that would kind of ruin the surprise. That left one option, and Jake cringed when it occurred to him. He slowly got out his phone.

Jake: Hey, how's it going?
Chip: Awesome. Straight chilling!
Jake: Sweet. Hey, I was wondering if you had Graham's address.
Chip: What? Why?
Jake: I need it. Please?

Chip: You told me to stop giving people addresses.
Jake: Though I'm glad you were listening, I said to stop giving people *my* address. Do you have his?
Chip: Wait, are you going to pull a Graham and show up on his doorstep??!!
Jake: Yeah.
Chip: You guys are such dorks. Okay, let me find it.

An eternity passed before Chip came back with the address. Jake immediately copied it into his maps app. He was about an hour away. Oh God. He was going to see Graham, and soon. He flipped back to his conversation with Chip.

Jake: Thank you, seriously.
Chip: Have fun. Don't do anything I wouldn't do!!!!

Since Jake couldn't imagine what the limits of Chip's boundaries were, he just responded with a smiley face emoji.

Chip: BTW, that J.R. guy returned the money I sent him.
Jake: Seriously? Why?
Chip: IDK. Maybe he really likes your mom?

Jake had three seconds to contemplate that semi-disturbing but also sweet sentiment before getting Chip's next text.

Chip: She must be smokin'. Send pics!!!!!!

Jake didn't bother to respond. He signed off and got back in the truck. He couldn't believe it, but he kind of owed Chip now, and spent the rest of the drive contemplating how he could repay the favor instead of obsessing over what he was going to say when he saw Graham again. Maybe they wouldn't be doing much talking.

A guy could hope.

GRAHAM'S NEIGHBORHOOD WAS NICE. The charming, tree-lined street almost made the horrible traffic and three wrong turns Jake had taken to get there worth it. Why did whoever designed the roads in Boston decide to put the signs *after* the exits?

Anyway, it appeared he'd made it, because he spotted Graham's Civic parked on the street outside of number 14. It was a townhouse, split into three apartments. Graham had the top floor. Jake got what he'd said about not having room for a dog. There was barely any yard; what he could see of one had a grill and what looked half a dozen bicycles chained up, occupying a lot of the available real estate. Still, the vibe of the place was urban New England at its best, colorfully painted exteriors glinting in the spring sunshine.

Jake parked his truck a few doors down. He might have been a little close to a fireplug, but hopefully it wouldn't garner him a ticket. He'd made good time, and now he shuffled from foot to foot indecisively on the sidewalk under a leafy green maple. It was edging toward evening, but that didn't mean Graham was home. He'd told him that today's track meet was all-day and at a school some distance away. Maybe he should go get some food, have it waiting when Graham arrived home. Or maybe Graham would go get food with his fellow coaches or a friend and he wouldn't be home for hours and Jake's *surprise-my-long-distance-boyfriend* plan was dumb and he should just go.

A white Jeep pulled up in front of number 14 and idled in the street. Jake watched as someone got out of the passenger side. Someone with sandy brown hair and green eyes and an athletic bag slung over his shoulder. Graham. He saluted a goodbye to whoever had dropped him off, then walked to the front of the townhouse.

Jake had to remind himself to walk toward Graham instead of just ogle him from twenty feet away like an inept stalker. Graham hadn't spotted him yet. He was getting his keys out of the pocket of his mud-smeared track pants, his shoulders rounded by fatigue. He looked so breathtakingly good, Jake actually forgot to breathe.

But then the door was opening and Jake croaked, "Graham."

His boyfriend whipped his head around, dropping his bag onto the mat in front of the door. "Jake?"

He closed the distance between them in two large strides. He'd had words prepared, but he didn't need them. Graham lunged for him, wrapping his strong arms around Jake's shoulders and pulling him close. Jake went willingly, melting into Graham's embrace, wrapping his own octopus arms around Graham's waist, reveling in feeling his strong, beautiful boyfriend's body against his.

They hugged for a minute, until Jake worried the

hard on he was developing would ruin the mood, and shifted away. "Hi."

"Hi. Jake, what are you doing here? I'm so—I'm so glad you are." Graham's eyes were rimmed red. Maybe them being apart had been just as hard on Graham as it had been on Jake. Somehow, he'd assumed that he was the needy one, moping around because Graham was far away while Graham was off living his best life. Maybe he'd been wrong.

"Can I come in?"

"Of course, yeah. Please." Graham picked up his bag and took his keys out of the lock. Jake closed the door behind them and followed Graham up a flight of stairs, past a door marked A. They went up a second flight, and another door marked B. By the time they reached the top floor and the door marked C, Jake was feeling his breath. "Now I know how you keep in shape," he remarked.

Graham smiled as he unlocked his door. "I'm used to it, but yeah." He paused before they went in. "I can't believe you're here. Like, honestly, I can't believe it. How did you even know where to find me?"

"Believe it or not, Chip." Jake grinned at the surprised look on Graham's face. "He called me showing up here 'pulling a Graham.'"

Graham chuckled and pushed the door open all the way. "Fair enough." When they were both inside with the door firmly shut behind them, he leaned in and kissed Jake with a week's worth of pent-up longing. Jake felt the kiss down to his toes. "I'm so glad you did, babe," Graham whispered.

"Me, too." They kissed their way to the living room.

Graham pulled him down so they were both on the couch, Jake half-under Graham, who had barely let up his assault on Jake's mouth. Not that he was complaining, but it was hard to talk about the tough things they needed to talk about when their mouths were otherwise occupied.

It was Graham who stopped first, tearing himself away from Jake with a groan, putting a foot or so of space between them as he scooted as far back as the tiny couch would allow. "Sorry. Got carried away. You're a good kisser."

"I am?" Jake was astonished.

"Yeah. You really commit. It's hot."

"Who wouldn't be committed in a kiss with you?" Jake honestly wanted to know.

"I'm all dirty from the meet. I should shower. We should order some food, too. I have nothing in the fridge. Or we could go out?" Graham bit his lip. "It's just—wow, I can't believe you're here."

"You said that already." Jake smiled. He knew he'd made the right decision to rearrange his schedule and make this trip. He and Graham were at the beginning of something special, and he wanted to give them the best possible start. Which is why he wanted to tell Graham the decision he'd come to. "I don't care about you showering. You smell amazing, but you can if you want. As for food, I guess we should eat, but there are things I want to say first. Or if not first, then soon."

"Okay." Graham shot him a slightly apprehensive look. "Good things?"

"I hope so," Jake answered honestly.

Graham relaxed a fraction. "Then maybe you could order the food while I take a shower?"

Tasks duly assigned, Graham handed Jake a menu from a diner around the corner, then went down a short hallway off the living room to the bathroom. Jake could hear the water turn on as if Graham were in the same room. He noticed for the first time just how small the place was. The kitchen was efficiency-style, with a smaller than average stove and a mini-fridge. The microwave, also small, was set on top of what was presumably the table where Graham ate his meals—two folding chairs stuck underneath the small wooden table-top. The living room was clean and tidy, and held the small couch and a coffee table with Graham's laptop closed on top of it. No TV. What little space was left held shelves full of books, some DVDs.

His gaze caught on a couple of photos in frames on the top of one bookshelf. He stood up and peered at the pictures without disturbing them. One was of an older couple—a man and a woman—squinting into the sun in front of a single-story ranch-style house. A Texas flag hung from their front porch. Graham's parents? The second was of a smiling man with three days of stubble on his appealing, strong-jawed face. There were two long smile lines carved into his cheeks that matched his dancing brown eyes. He had to be Mitch.

Jake swallowed hard. He reminded himself that Mitch was an important part of Graham's past, but that they were both focusing on the future. He looked down at the menu in his hands, called the diner and placed an order for two burgers and fries for delivery.

The water shut off, and Jake kept himself from helping Graham dry off personally by perusing the books on his shelves. He spotted a few of his favorites—*Ready Player One* and *Jurassic Park* among them. There was a lot of fantasy and science fiction. He froze when he saw a paperback titled *Promise Me Tomorrow*. The author was Jeremy Robinson, Jr.

He shook his head in disbelief and pulled it from the shelf, paging through it. There was no picture of the author, but he knew this was his mom's paramour's novel. What were the odds? He sat on the couch and had read most of the first surprisingly engrossing chapter by the time Graham emerged from the bathroom dressed in a clean tee and sweats, his hair damp, looking squeaky clean and mouthwateringly good. He was even wearing his glasses.

Jake let the book slide out of his hands. "You are so freaking attractive. It's unreal."

"What's unreal is that you're in my apartment, all huge and sexy. I forgot how big you are." Graham walked to the couch, slid to his knees onto the floor in front of Jake. "What are you wearing, gorgeous?"

Jake glanced at his button-down. It was a simple dark blue shirt, but new. He'd gone shopping a couple of days ago for some non-flannel apparel. It was a slimmer fit than he was used to. He'd been hiding under baggy sizes, trying to camouflage himself and what he'd been convinced were abnormally long appendages. But then Graham had come, and called him gorgeous, and made him *feel* gorgeous, and it had seemed only right to honor that with new clothes.

"You like this?" Jake asked unnecessarily. He could see Graham's admiration in his eyes, magnified by his sexy-as-hell glasses.

"Yeah. Shows off your broad shoulders and your sexy little waist." His hands slid up to said waist, and he shuffled forward on his knees until he was framed by Jake's thighs. Graham tipped his head up and closed his eyes. What was Jake supposed to do if not lean down and kiss him?

They made out until Jake knocked into Graham's glasses one too many times. Apparently, he needed practice making out with a guy in glasses. The text from the delivery person letting Jake know they were downstairs arrived a minute later. They broke apart, adjusting themselves in their pants. Jake jogged downstairs while Graham stayed behind to get out plates and silverware.

When Jake arrived back at the top floor with the food, Graham asked, "You want something to drink? I have beer, water, um, expired milk?"

Jake said beer was fine, left Graham to the kitchen. If he'd tried to help, they would have gotten immediately tangled up in the small space.

"So, your place is nice," Jake said from the safety of the living room. "You been here long?"

"Since grad school. I kept telling myself I'd move when I got my teaching job, then after I got my teaching job, I figured I'd move after I had some money saved, but I'm still here."

"Inertia," Jake said. "I know something about that."

Graham handed him a beer and they sat at the table

and unloaded their burgers and fries onto plates. "But you seem like you're making some changes now."

"Overdue, but then again, maybe I was waiting for the right time."

Graham smiled at him. "I'm proud of you, Jake."

"Thanks." Jake looked at his burger. He was hungry, but this was important. "I've been doing a lot of thinking this past week. I know we're still early in this...well, what's between us." He felt his cheeks getting warm. "I mean, it's new, but it feels really good."

"Yeah."

Graham's soft agreement gave him courage.

"And I need to get my own place, but I was thinking, maybe I should move here. To Boston. Long distance is the worst, and we've only had to do it for a week. And maybe we'd get used to it, but I don't want to get used to it. I want to be with you. So, I thought, why not move here. And it doesn't have to be here, here—" Jake couldn't quite visualize how the two of them and their stuff could comfortably coexist in this space, which was kind of disappointing "—but near you. I want to be near you."

Graham put his burger down. He averted his gaze from Jake, looking somewhere in the microwave's vicinity. He bit his lip nervously, Jake thought.

"I don't think that's a good idea."

TWENTY

DISAPPOINTMENT LANCED through Jake sharp and swift, as if Graham had taken an actual lance and carelessly run him through. He hadn't wanted to overstep, to rush Graham, but he'd figured they were on the same page, that Graham would be open to the idea of them living in the same city, if not the same apartment.

But no matter how happy Graham had appeared to be when Jake arrived, there were limits to their relationship. Of course, Graham was older. He had more experience. He probably thought Jake wanting to move to be near him within a week after meeting each other for the first time was nuts—and he was likely right.

The only thing he could think to say was, "Oh." Jake could deal. He'd be an adult about this—isn't that what he'd been trying to do since Graham arrived in his life? Adulting and all that crap? He'd pull himself together and be mature and yeah, maybe it felt slightly like being run over by a lawnmower, but that's what Nana had said.

Being an adult sucked. If Graham wanted things to move slower, he could handle that.

"You're right—" he said just as Graham started talking again.

"Here's the thing—" Graham broke off when he realized Jake was speaking.

They looked at each other. Jake felt his mouth turn down at the corners. Graham was drumming his fingers on the table.

"It's a bad idea," Jake said, when Graham didn't rush to fill the silence. "I get it. You're right—I don't know what I was thinking. We basically just met and I'm being totally—"

"No!" Graham exclaimed. He reached across the little table and grabbed Jake's forearm. His lips pursed with distress. "Is that what you thought? No, I'm so—no. That's not what I meant."

Jake was super confused. He felt like he and Graham had been here before—communication wasn't always their strong suit. He took a deep breath and said as evenly as possible, "Can you please tell me what you did mean, then?"

"I wasn't sure how to tell you about this, because I thought maybe you would think I was being presumptuous, but...." Graham swallowed nervously.

Jake was distracted for a split second by the sexy bob of Graham's Adam's apple, but then shook himself out of it. "I swear to God, if you don't spit it out I'm going to—eat all your fries!"

Graham cracked a smile and held up a protective hand

over his pile of fries. "Okay. I'm sorry. I did two things this week that I haven't told you about yet, but considering what you just said, well, here goes: I applied for a couple of jobs. One at Apple Vale High School. One at the middle school in Henderson. I think it's like a twenty-minute drive?"

Jake nodded. Henderson was the town where Singer's Steakhouse was located.

"I also found this place. It's a rental, but it looks cute in the pictures. A two-bedroom house with a yard. Pet-friendly. It's on Macoun Street, kind of near the train station. Maybe you know it?"

Of all the things he'd expected Graham to say, those weren't on the list. He'd seen the house when he was looking for apartments, discarding it as too big and too expensive for one person, as much as he liked the area and the idea of having room for a dog.

"If one of the jobs comes through, I'll put in notice at my school. Hell, I think I will anyway. I'll find something eventually. I don't have anything else tying me to Boston. This place is on a month-to-month lease." Graham looked around the minuscule apartment. "I could move in about a month, easy as anything." His gaze returned to Jake. "Especially if I had a big, tall, strong man helping me move."

"You are unbelievable."

Graham frowned. "Huh?"

"I was all worried about suggesting I move closer to you, and you've been looking at houses with yards? Are you kidding me?" Jake took a slightly perverse sense of satisfaction in the way Graham shifted nervously in his chair after the mental and emotional gymnastics he'd just put him through. "And what are you going to do with all that room, huh?"

Graham bit his lip. "I thought maybe you'd want to, um, move in together. You said you hadn't found a place yet."

Jake thrilled with the invitation and the serious way Graham issued it, but he wasn't ready to let his boyfriend off the hook quite yet. "Why would you want to move to Apple Vale? It's nothing special."

"Besides you being there?" Graham asked.

Jake nodded, trying not to let on just how sweet he found the sentiment.

Graham held up fingers as he listed out reasons. "I've been in Boston for too long. I was going to leave years ago and I never did. It's time for a change. Also, I need a bigger place, clearly. I like Apple Vale, it reminds me of where I grew up. It's got a cool car show and nearby is my new favorite steakhouse. And it has you, Jake, my new favorite person. You have so much there—your family, your volunteer work. Why should I make you leave those things when I'd be honored to move there and become a part of your community? I found the person I want to build a life with. It's you, Jake. And yeah, we could build that life here. But you already have a life. Let me come be a part of it. Please."

Graham touched Jake's arm and looked at him, face open, the love in his heart shining out of his gorgeous green eyes.

Jake wanted to say so much, but maybe Graham had said it all. So he kept it simple. "Yes."

"Yes?" Graham's lips curved a little, as if he was holding back until he was sure.

"Yes. Let's move into a house together and get a dog and be sickeningly happy."

Graham's lips went full-grin. Jake felt himself smiling back just as hard. They stared at each other like lovestruck fools until Jake's cheeks ached. "Okay, we either need to eat or have sex," he said.

"We need fuel to give us the stamina for all the things I want to do with you," Graham said, picking up his burger and waggling his eyebrows meaningfully.

Jake had no problem with that plan.

MUCH LATER, after exchanging blow jobs to take the edge off, Jake was lying on his side in Graham's bed, naked and idly stroking his semi-hard cock while Graham, wearing only his glasses, was working lube-covered fingers into his own ass.

They'd talked about it, and Graham was down for anything, but he'd convinced Jake that for their first time he should top. Jake had only agreed because he knew they'd have a chance to try everything eventually, and while he was very much looking forward to feeling Graham inside him at his soonest possible convenience, he had to admit, watching Graham open himself up, knowing his cock was going to be replacing his fingers and get sucked up into Graham's tantalizing hole was making him lightheaded with desire.

Before long, his cock was fully hard, and Graham had

worked up to three fingers. "It's been a while for me," Graham panted. "And you're, well, not small. Give me another minute." He reapplied lube and wriggled a fourth finger in, shallow but persistent. Jake could only imagine how it felt, and he had to stop touching himself until he regained control.

"You are so fucking hot, Graham."

"I'm almost ready," he said. "You want me like this?" He was propped up on pillows, his feet planted flat on the bed, his cock, balls, and hole on display as he pumped his fingers in and out steadily.

Jake definitely wanted to see his mind-meltingly hot boyfriend's face while he entered him, but—"Whatever you want."

"Let's try it, babe. I want to see you."

Jake's heart swelled. They really were on the same page about most things when they could actually manage to communicate.

"Me too," he said softly.

A moment later, Graham nodded, wiped his hand on a tissue, then beckoned Jake closer. He inched forward between Graham's legs. The bed creaked and groaned under their combined weight as they moved. "We're going to use my bed in our place," Jake said, rolling a condom on with only slightly shaky fingers. "What is this, a double?"

"It's a queen," Graham said, a bit defensively. "But yeah, it feels smaller with you in it, Stretch."

Jake ignored that, kissed him. "You ready?"

"So ready," Graham said.

He took Jake's wrapped cock in hand, helped him position it. Jake edged forward. He was a little scared of hurting Graham, no matter how much prep he'd done. "Let me know if—"

"I will. It's okay. Keep going."

Jake took it slow, the blunt head of his cock finding the lube-slick channel. The tight heat, the intense intimacy, overwhelmed him. He was going to be inside Graham. Actually, he was already inside Graham. They were joined together, and it felt impossibly wonderful. Graham tipped his hips up, guiding Jake deeper.

"Yeah, that's good, babe. So good. So big. So full." Graham's sounded wrecked, but not in pain. "There's more?" A touch of wonder in his voice.

Jake looked down and nodded. The sight of his cock disappearing into Graham's hole was the hottest thing he'd ever seen.

"Keep going," Graham ordered sweetly.

Jake obeyed until he was fully inside the man he loved. He stilled, reveling in the feeling of being so deep. "God, Graham."

"I know. Can you move?"

Jake pulled out almost entirely, his arms shaking with the effort of holding himself up and hanging onto his control. "Okay?"

"Hang on, more lube," Graham said. He grabbed the already-open bottle from the table by the bed and dribbled more onto Jake's cock. The lube was cool compared to the heat of Graham's body, and it smoothed the way as Jake bottomed out again, faster this time.

Graham's groan was filthy and beautiful. "Yes, again," and Jake was helpless to do anything but what Graham asked. They found a rhythm, and all too soon, Graham's hands on his own dick caused him to arch up, coming without warning all over his chest and belly, the clench of his ass around Jake's dick almost making him go off, too, but he managed a few more strokes before the sight of Graham's blissed out face, his pink cheeks and pouty lips forming the silent words, "I love you," pushed him into an orgasm that had him filling the condom with a shout.

He pulled out while holding onto the condom. He wrapped it in a tissue that Graham thoughtfully handed to him. They used more tissues to mop themselves up, then lay back down on the too-small bed. Graham threw himself onto Jake's chest, nuzzling into his neck. "You are really good at that."

"Really?" Jake had gone on instinct mostly, but it helped that Graham had guided him through it. "You helped me."

"I think more practice is going to perfect something that's already working pretty great."

"I can't believe we're going to be living together. We'll be able to do that all the time."

Graham huffed out a laugh. "When we aren't working and eating and walking the dog."

"The dog," Jake repeated. "What should we name it?"

"Well, since we're getting a dog from the shelter, I assume it will already have a name."

Jake kissed the top of Graham's head. "I love you."

"I love you, too." Graham kissed Jake's neck. "You know, I've spent this week wondering how I got so lucky that the guy I've been pining for for so long turned out to be a gorgeous man who loves me back. It's you, Jake. It's been you for years."

Jake didn't think his heart could hold more love for the man in his arms, but he was wrong. "Nana said she thought one reason I stayed single for so long was because I was waiting for the right person. She says hi by the way."

"Hi, Nana."

Jake smiled and went on. "She was right. Because the moment I met you online, three years ago, I didn't want anyone else. And now that I have you, I know I'm never going to want anyone else. You're it for me, Graham."

"So we're both lucky."

"The luckiest," Jake agreed. And they fell asleep wrapped up in their love, their good fortune, and each other.

"DO WE HAVE ENOUGH ICE? I feel like we don't have enough ice. Maybe I should get more ice." Graham bounced up and down on the balls of his feet as Jake dumped another bag of chips into a bowl. The bar separating their kitchen from their living room was covered in food—chips, salsa, guacamole that Jake had made himself, plus pretty much every kind of appetizer the local deli counter had had on offer. On the other side of the bar were two coolers, one full of beer, another of soft drinks, and they were both filled to the brim with ice.

Jake laughed and kissed his boyfriend's shoulder. "We have plenty of ice, Graham. I think you need to relax. This is going to be fun."

"I know. You'd think I never had a housewarming party before. Wait. I never have had a housewarming party before."

Jake laughed again. Graham was so cute when he was nervous. "Me, either. But no one we invited is expecting anything major. We have tons of food, drinks, and yes, ice. Put on the music, and we're set."

After spending their first night in their new place two weeks earlier, they had officially unpacked the last box last night, and celebrated by jerking each other off in the kitchen, which meant they'd officially had sex in every room in their house. Of course, they'd be keeping that bit of information to themselves. His mom didn't need to know that they'd already fucked on the brand-new couch she and his aunts had gotten together to buy for them.

Speaking of Liv, she was probably going to be their first guest. The doorbell rang. Graham froze. "I don't know if I can do this."

"Hey, look at me." Jake tilted Graham's chin up. "It's going to be fine. It's casual. Just people dropping by to wish us well and bring us presents. They're happy for us. I'm happy for us. Aren't you happy for us, Graham?"

"So happy," Graham whispered. Jake could see the truth of it in his heart-stoppingly beautiful face.

Jake dropped a quick kiss to Graham's lips and went to open the door. Liv was, predictably, on the welcome mat. But she wasn't alone. Jeremy Robinson, Junior, was at her side. They were holding hands.

"Hi, guys!" Jake opened the door wide, gave his mom a kiss on the cheek, and waved cheerfully at Jeremy. He was still getting used to the idea of his mom in a serious relationship, but it could have been worse. Jeremy was cool. And he was a pretty good writer, too. Jake had borrowed Graham's copy of *Promise Me Tomorrow* and read it in two days. Graham had been intrigued when Jake explained why he wanted to borrow the book, since he'd loved it and hadn't realized two others in the series had already come out. Jake had bought them online and had them sent to Graham's apartment to give him something to pass the time until their, thankfully numbered, days of long distance were over.

"We brought wine." Liv held up a bottle of chardonnay.

"And ice—it's blazing hot today," Jeremy added, holding up a plastic bag.

"Graham, come take this," Jake called with a smile in his voice.

When Graham appeared at his side, he looked at Jeremy's offering. "Ice, oh man, I love you!"

Jake chuckled. "Yeah, he's not usually this easy, but for some reason he's fixated on ice. Graham, you remember my mom's boyfriend, Jeremy?"

Graham flushed scarlet. "I'm a fan," he said quickly, then took the bag and ran away to hide in the kitchen.

Jake only had time to direct his mom and Jeremy to the food and drinks when the doorbell sounded again. A steady stream of people arrived after that, Carrie and Sarah and a few other people from the animal shelter, several of his acquaintances at the nursing home. Nana arrived with another resident, Bill, who Jake had met a few times, but hadn't realized was such a good friend of his grandmother's. He watched them together for a few moments; Bill was attentive and brought Nana a sparkling water, and Nana laughed at one of Bill's jokes in such a way that Jake could see that love may have struck three generations of Cranes at once.

Liana from the diner arrived. She and Graham had

become friends, bonding over Graham's instant and deep love of the Apple Pan's apple fritters. Carlos, the head of the mental health services department of the county hospital where Jake had just started working, came with his partner, Eliza, who was a doctor at the hospital.

Their house was feeling very packed indeed when Graham surprised him by clanging a fork on his bottle of beer to get everyone's attention.

"I just wanted to say thank you to everyone for coming and giving me such a warm welcome to Apple Vale, and such a warm start to our first home together." Everyone made appreciative noises. Graham went on, "And I have good news—in the fall I'll be teaching computer science and math at Apple Vale High School, and I'll be assistant coaching the track team, too."

There was a chorus of congratulations and Jake was smiling so hard he was afraid his cheeks might split. Graham had only gotten the call about the job yesterday, and he was so proud of him. He was also impressed, as an alum of Apple Vale High, that Graham had declared his intention to take on the culture there, to make sure any kid who identified as queer wouldn't feel as alone as Jake had when he was a student there.

"Also, thanks for the all the booze." Everyone laughed because bottles of every type had seemed to be the house-warming gift of choice. Graham stepped off the prover-bial stage, and the party resumed around them.

"Nice job," Jake said, squeezing Graham's arm.

Graham leaned into Jake's side. "Thanks, babe."

"Good turnout, huh?" He honestly couldn't believe how many people had come to support them.

"You're pretty popular," Graham said.

Jake chuckled, then his chuckle turned into a full-blown laugh as he realized what Graham had said.

"What's so funny?"

"Just—you're right. I spent so many years feeling alone. My dad told me I wasn't, that I wouldn't be, and I didn't believe him, but I should have." Jake wiped his eyes, which had suddenly begun to water. He looked at the amazing, beautiful love of his life. "I have to thank you, Graham. It wasn't until you came into my life and showed me how it felt to be loved romantically that I could understand I already had a lot of other kinds of love in my life."

Graham's eyes looked watery, too. "You are loved, Jake. By so many people."

"I know that now." Jake sighed with so much happiness and goodwill toward every single person who loved him, whether they were here today or not. His dad, especially. Even Chip, lovable lunatic that he was. "I'm glad that I finally figured out I already had it pretty good before you came along. You're my icing on the cake. Or my strawberries on the cheesecake, maybe."

"Babe, I'm honored to be the strawberries on top of the cheesecake of your life." Graham licked his lips.

Jake imagined feeding Graham strawberries and then licking the sweet taste out of his mouth. "Hold that thought until our house isn't crowded with people, okay?"

"I can do that," Graham said, a smirk forming on his face.

Carrie from the shelter walked up to them, and Jake took a reluctant step back from his boyfriend, tamping down on the lascivious thoughts running through his head.

"You guys! This place is so cute. And I noticed you have a fenced-in backyard. I assume your lease allows for pets?" Carrie had an expectant look on her face.

"It does. We were actually going to see if—"

She didn't wait for him to finish. "Then I have great news! Rocky's new owners unexpectedly didn't work out, and he's back at the shelter. I know how much you two bonded, Jake, and I thought I'd ask if—"

"Yes!" Jake said.

"We'd love him," Graham agreed simultaneously.

"That's what I was hoping you'd say. Can you stop by tomorrow to fill out the paperwork? I think we can expedite things for you."

"We'll be there." Jake looked at Graham. "Oh my God, we're going to get Rocky."

"Our dog." Graham grinned and raised his drink. "To Rocky."

"To us," Jake added, as they clinked their bottles together.

"To us."

Thanks for reading!

For a bonus story featuring Jake and Graham that ends in another happy ending, plus more feel-good, small-town romances, get Elle's collection *His Ever After* now!

ABOUT THE AUTHOR

Fueled by chocolate and canned wine, Elle Waters writes smutty small town romance with guaranteed happy endings. She lives with her family in Connecticut. Sign up for her newsletter at ellewatersauthor.com to hear about her next release!

Elle loves to hear from readers at elle@ ellewatersauthor.com.

facebook.com/ElleWatersAuthor

instagram.com/ellewatersbooks

amazon.com/~/e/B091FZQ4PZ

bookbub.com/authors/elle-waters

reamstories.com/ellewaters